Th Weirdish Wild Space

JOE CASSIUS

The 93rd Greatest Novel of All-Time

THE CHOIR PRESS

Copyright © 2024 Joe Cassius

All rights reserved. No part of this publication may be reproduced or transmitted in any form or by any means, electronic or mechanical including photocopying, recording or any information storage or retrieval system, without prior permission in writing from the publishers.

The right of Joe Cassius to be identified as the author of this work has been asserted by him in accordance with the Copyright, Designs and Patents Act 1988

First published in the United Kingdom in 2024 by
The Choir Press

ISBN 978-1-78963-467-9

Contents

Introduction	v
I Couldn't Find It So I Created It	1
This Weirdish Wild Space	79
Chloe's Calf	87
A Happy Orphan	185
An Audience of One	237
Swayze Dayz	253

Introduction

By Joe Archer

I first met Joe Cassius back in the year 2024/25, just after the publication of his debut novel *This Weirdish Wild Space*.

The previous year had seen the publication of my own debut. Some 200,000 word slog of a book. In many ways our novels are set at opposite sides of the spectrum.

Mine – a sleeping giant with a small, humble audience.

His – a wafer-thin slip of a thing, but which blazed through the universe to absolute apocalyptic proportions.

Joe Cassius.

How or why he ever decided to meet me at this time, I'll never know. Call it luck. Call it pity. Call it God.

Of course on the morning of meeting him my nerves were nothing short of catastrophic, catatonic.

Coffee with Cassius, WTF!

Who is this man, what should I expect?

Working from the clues, fingerprints and DNA of his novel, and its hero which voyages through *these* pages, I was expecting a swashbuckling sexy pirate, or maybe an introverted version – some brooding silent shadow of a stranger.

Cooler than you. Bigger than me. Larger than life.

So you can imagine my surprise, if not shock, when this small, shy, unsure, Caribbean gentleman shuffled out from behind the curtain. Greying and balding, holding himself together with envelope neatness, a too-soft voice cradling a faraway accent.

He was not the man I was expecting. He is not the man any of us are expecting.

A simple man with everyday tastes.

Tender and taciturn. Intensely private, sacrificially humble. This is Joe Cassius.

We met again in 2048, just months before his death. I was happier because on this occasion I got to tell him just how crucial his novel was for me. How it had *literally* saved me from a literary death. Responsible for the resurrection of my prose and every novel I've written since.

"Oh Joe," he said, waving me off. "It's just my art."

Mr Cassius remained as he ever was. He really didn't see the big deal.

Back then, we as a human race didn't have the technological leaps of today. The phenomenon of Artisticology wasn't yet conceived. It was a primitive time where people actually judged art based on subjective whims and preferences. It was a wayward, barbaric period of arbitrary opinions and poor, self-indulgent judgements. Joe Cassius lived in this world and his work, *this* novel, his art as he called it, never truly reached these heights in his lifetime.

But...

along came Artisticology and changed all that. *This Weirdish Wild Space* was placed in the database along with every other novel ever written ... and out it came ... scientifically proven to be the 93rd Greatest Novel of All-Time.

Just WOW.

Just wild. Just justice.

My own debut *All is Wild, All is Silent* came in at a modest 4,666th.

But hey, ha,

I know my place. I know my lane. I know my limit. I accept my lot.

For JC there really is no limit. His talent touches the very top.

Amongst them now. Shoulder to shoulder with the likes of Wilde, Orwell, F. Scotty Fitz, and all those solemn Russian boys.

What he would have made of this I'm not entirely sure. He was an old-school man with an old-school way. A part of that old, old world and I'm not sure he would have approved of all this carry-on. Just as he waved off my praise chances are he would have waved off this too, making this immortal list, of the esteemed top-100.

Or...

maybe he looks down on us all with a silent pride, a boyish glee. Secretly and securely at peace with his anonymous genius. Whatever.

I know what this novel did for me and now you're gonna see what it's going to do for you.

So without any further ado, I hand it over, over to you.

You have it in your hands.

The Introduction is *almost* done and now you get to ride the wave.

Ride this wild horse through these weirdish lands.

So whoever you are and wherever you are –

treat yourself to the turning of another page,

and let's begin ...

Dedicated to You

"You can get so confused
that you'll start in to race
down long wiggled roads at a break-necking pace
and grind on for miles across weirdish wild space,
headed, I fear, toward a most useless place.
                              The Waiting Place..."

Dr. Seuss

Mum

died.

Dead.
Funeral.
Cool coffin.
Black, like a piano.
Shiny.
Can see my face in it.
Fuck I look good, sharp, *hot.*
The shape of my stubble is shark-like, *scintillating.*
Yep, since turning thirty my handsomeness has almost become offensive.
So glad I didn't check-out at 27 like I was going to.
So glad I stuck it out.
So glad I got to look after Mama.
She needed me.
No one else was around.
No one else was around to provide the goods.
I step forward and look at the rest of myself in the coffin.
Suits really suit me only I never get to wear them.
Court and funerals, that's it.
Never get invited to weddings.
Guess I just haven't got that face.
Of course everybody is crying, some hysterical.
Especially when they play the song at the end.
Diana Ross's *Touch Me in The Morning.*
It's not even the right fucking song.
It's the wrong fucking song.
The one she likes *(liked)* is *(was)* the one with Luther Vandross.
I kept telling Dad but he never listened.
Now it's on and I look at his confused, tear-drenched face and the penny drops ... *ah, this isn't the one?*
Straight away it's my fault.
I see it in his expression.
Blame.
Anger.
Hate, maybe.
I take a closer look.

Yep.

Hate's definitely there.

Here.

But then it always has been.

We start to file out from the pews.

All of us.

One by one.

Like a conga-line of zombies, shuffling from side to side like we've shit our pants.

Why do people walk like this in churches?

Like anything remotely self-assured could be interpreted as sexy, thus a sin.

Most of these peeps I don't even recognise.

Fat Aunt Audrey's fat face is still buried in her snotty handkerchief.

Funny cos five minutes ago she was like Liza Minnelli in *Cabaret* performing her rendition of the Dylan Thomas poem ... *Rage, rage against the dying of the light.*

Mum didn't even like poetry.

Mum didn't even read.

Not sure Mum even *could* read, not properly.

And she definitely wasn't raging against the dying of the light.

She couldn't wait to go.

Looked forward to it.

Craved the fucking thing.

We even joked about it.

She'd wake and look at me, disappointed.

"Not agaaain. What I wouldn't give to see a flat-line."

I'd pour her some smuggled-in wine and tell her to look on the *dark side.*

Ah, memories, I think.

A tear in my eye, almost.

By the door Dad is at me.

His face in mine.

"That wasn't the song."

"Tried telling you."

"I don't believe it. I don't fucking believe it."

He's walking around in circles, hyperventilating.

"She liked this little ditty too Pops. Relax."

Actually she wanted the 1980's classic *The Heat Is On* to be played as she rolled into the furnace.

He grabs my wrist and stares so hard I can see my reflection in his eyeballs.

"C'mon Ron."

Aunt Audrey comes to the rescue.

His rescue.

But Dad isn't done.

"You didn't even cry. And you're wearing *a hat*."

I touch my hat.

His face is shaking.

For a moment I envisage a cardiac.

Wonder if the parlour would do us a two-for-one deal?

"A hat at a funeral! Your *own* mother's funeral. Wearing a hat in church. So fucking disrespectful!"

The *fucking* seems to echo.

People look over.

It's then I see her for the first time.

Stepping from the pew with a flick of her blonde quiff.

At first I think it's a beautiful boy but then see my dyke cousin Megan next to her and realise it's the girlfriend.

Why am I nervous?

I'm never nervous, *ever*.

The feeling is so alien I wonder if I'm coming down with something.

She's the only one not crying, and seems to not have a care in the world to her girlfriend who is producing some impressive tears.

For a moment I think she could be a ghost.

Dad is still going ballistic about the song and I wonder if he's drunk.

"And you're not even coming back to the gathering are you?"

"I am now," I say, looking at her.

Hearse is cool.

And with the suit and everything I pretend I am Matthew McConaughey.

Taking a ride through the Hollywood Hills.

Sit like him and talk like him.

Feel him.

Become him.

Wild expressions.

Whistling Texan drawl.

"Where y'all goin now?"

We pull up at the social club that Dad has booked for the bash.

Now the peeps have stopped crying and are queuing at the bar like it's a Saturday night.

Epic spread on.

Sausage rolls n' Co.

Everyone is complimenting Aunt Aud on her poetry performance.

Laps it up like she's at the Oscars.

Giving a speech *about* her speech.

In the gents I take off my hat and take out my wax and fix my hair.

Matt wouldn't wear a hat.

Back in the hall I look out for Megan and her ghost of a girlfriend.

Again that weird feeling wriggles in my gut so I sit.

Then it happens like it always does.

The people.

They come.

They come to me.

I don't do anything or say anything but they flock like crows at feeding time.

I'd be lying if I said I didn't like it.

I'd be lying if I said I did.

Like is not the word.

Love is the word.

Adore.

Revel.

Thrive.

For some reason they want my attention.

Need.

Crave.

Compete.

I am pulled and prodded.

Hugged.

Kissed.

Squeezed.

It's always been this way.

The less I do the more they want.

People look at me, amazed.

I feel like Matthew McConaughey again.

Chew gum.

Comb back my hair with two hands.

Occasionally I'll wink at someone.

By the time my glass is empty it is replaced with a full.

Before I know it hours have passed and the DJ has become a good friend of mine.

Gone is all that morbid Motown shit.

Dad trying to right the wrong by having Ross and Vandross playing on *re-peat*.

Blurred Lines bounces from the speakers and I hit the floor, ring around me.

Hat back on, cocked.

McConaughey subbed for Timberlake.

I move.

Clicking to the beat.

Spin on my heels.

Sideways like a crab, Moonwalk.

Crowd go wild.

Clap.

Cheer.

Chant.

"This is what Barb would have wanted," I hear someone say.

I dance with Aunt Aud.

My sister.

Linda.

Kathy.

Sylvia.

June.

Swinging from one old dear to another.

Feel like *Magic Mike* and almost whip off my shirt.

Only I see Dad slumped alone in the corner and really I should show some respect.

By now I'm dancing with Megan, her funeral shirt open to an AC/DC vest.

"You're incredible!" she screams through the music.

"Why?"

"Only you could turn this into something beautiful. It's what your mum would have wanted."

"I'm putting the *fun* back into funeral."

"Ha!"

"Where's your girlfriend?" I shout.
"Powdering her nose."
"Powdering her nose-powdering her nose?"
Slaps my arm, "You're so funny."
"Introduce me."
"She's shy."
"She's high?"
"SHY."
"Oh."
"She doesn't really talk."
"Oh."
"But I like that. Mysterious, y' know?"
"How long you been going out?"
"Coupla months."
"What's her name?"

Megan stops dancing and pulls my shirt. "Since when did you get so interested in my love life?"

"You're my favourite cousin."

Rolls her eyes. "I'm your *only* cousin."

"Ha."

"To be honest you're about the only one here who isn't a homophobic motherfucker."

"Really?"

"No offence. I know it's not really the time or the place and I know he's upset but your dad is rude."

"Ah don't mind him. He's just old school."

"Chloe."

"What?"

"My girlfriend's name is Chloe."

"Get her on the dance floor."

"Ah-ah. No way. You'll have to come to *her*."

"Well alright then."

"But don't start any of that rock star crap. She's shy."

It kind of goes quiet and in slow-motion as I walk up to the seated girl.

She's looking at the floor.

Hand across her mouth.

"Babe," Megan shouts.

And then she does that exact same flick of the quiff that she did in the church.

Looks at me, right at me, into me.

Blue eyes.

"This is my cousin."

Hold out my hand and she takes it, just.

"Hi," I say.

Her smile surprises me.

"Megan has just been telling you about me. I mean, telling *me* about *you*."

Still no words.

"You're Chloe."

She nods.

"Aren't you going to say something like *I'm sorry for your loss*?"

She looks at the party behind me, then back at my face.

I no longer feel like Matthew McConaughey.

Or Timberlake.

It's like she can read my mind.

You

"This Weirdish Wild Space," I say on sliding into your bedroom.

I flick the front cover of the book you're reading. "Hell of a fucking title."

You don't make a sound but I know you can hear me, *feel* me. Your breathing has changed and you wiggle your toes, a little. Maybe you can smell my aftershave, mingled with the natural pheromones of my strong, masculine scent. It beats through the room and enters your world, nose, brain, mind, spirit. Stirs your blood and wakes your body. Makes those blotches break out on your neck, one by one like rosebuds blooming, spreading across your chest and shoulders, before working its way down.

I unclip my watch and toss it onto the bedside table.

The straw chair you're sitting on creaks as you reposition yourself, focusing your eyes on *these very words*. You're onto chapter 2 now and already you realise that Joe Archer was right in his introduction, this really is starting to look like some kind of masterpiece.

"Not going to ask how my funeral went?" I say.

"*Your* funeral?" You reply in the smallest of voices, eyes momentarily darting up off this page, landing on my chest. "You're still alive. I can see you."

"Yeah I'm real," I say with a chuckle, chair dipping at the pressure of my knee.

"I'm reading," You say.

"I can see that," I reply, tracing a finger over the soft curve of your heel and up onto your calf. No contact though.

"Stop that," You say.

Blotches have made their way onto your legs now, thighs, shins. Your kneecap looks like a glowing Stop Light.

"Is it good?" I say.

"What?"

"Your book."

You put a little finger in your mouth and nod.

Cup your shoulder into the palm of my hand. "I'm almost a little jealous of this …" I bend down to take a closer look at the author's name. "… Joe Cassius guy … taking all your attention from me."

Still you read on so I give that shoulder a light squeeze.

"Let me finish this chapter," You say, determined.

I concede and step back, flick off my hat with one hand and catch it with the other, before lightly skimming it across the room. Hangs in the air like a Frisbee, and then that perfect hook on the back of the door.

"You should have seen me tonight babe," I say with a deep sigh. "I was fucking electric."

Kick off my shoes and fall heavy on the bed, gaze dreamily at the ceiling, replaying it all.

"The people. They were all over me. It was ridiculous."

The open window allows a breeze to make the curtain move, tickle your feet, cooling my face, dabbing at my eyes like a damp flannel. After a moment or two I look up at you; still reading, still lost in your book, *this* novel. Joe Cassius has all your attention and I guess I've just got to accept that.

"Baby I'm getting in bed," I say.

You nod, blink, feel this crisp page between your thumb and forefinger.

"I'm done," You say, standing slowly but your eyes are still buried deep within *these words*. "I'm done," You say again, lip folded behind your teeth as these final sentences glide on by like trickles of water. "I'm done," You say a third time, middle of the page now but tempted to turn it and start the next chapter, chapter **Dad.**

Dad

died.

Suicide.
Quite impressed actually.
Didn't think the old boy had it in him.
Someone found him hanging-out in the garage.
Always had Dad down for a jumper.
Definitely the blaze of glory type.
Drama, adrenalin, sprinkle of heroism.
That's him.
Was him.
Uncle broke the news, came over Monday morning, white as a ghost.
"I don't know how to tell you this?"
That's always the punchline for a death.
I don't know how to tell you this.
He didn't have to.
Read it in his face.
He may as well have had the corpse slung over his shoulder.
People say I don't understand emotion but they're wrong.
I see it a mile off.
I know emotion *very* well.
I put my head in my hands and started to cry.
But then realised I'd fucked up because he hadn't told me yet.
Probably thought I was psychic.
Or put him up to it in some way (no pun).
Got him the rope and gave the foot-stool a kick.
Uncle put a hairy arm around me and proceeded to console.
I had him in for a cup of tea and he gave me the deets:
Time.
Place.
Methodology.
Reactions.
"Want some biscuits to dunk Unc?"
Looked at me, then at the tea, back at me again, hurt, flash of anger.
See, *emotions*, I see them.
"No thanks," he said, gazing out the window.

Before he goes on I remembered something and my heart skipped a beat.

"When's the funeral?"

"Erm, well, we've only just…"

"Think your daughter will be going?"

Looked at me confused.

"Megan, yes, of course."

"What about her girlfriend, Chloe I think her name is?"

Unc didn't dig that his daught was a dyke.

And this clearly showed in his face.

"Erm, probably. Are you in shock?"

"I am," I said, dunking a digestive. "Shock."

Hands slid down his thighs, stopping at knees.

"I'm going to leave you alone."

"Okay," I said.

As he closed the gate he turned and looked at me.

"He died of a broken heart."

"I know," I said, watching his bald-patch hover over the hedge.

Car door.

Slam.

He drove away.

Even the engine sounded tragic.

Died of a broken heart.

It wasn't a broken heart that killed him.

It was a rope and a foot-stool.

It wasn't even a broken heart that lead him there.

It was guilt.

Despite his morals and principles and traditional ways Dad was having an affair, for years.

Kept it hidden.

Kept it hidden well.

Fooled them all.

All but me.

I see *everything*.

It was the smallest of things that gave him away too, *a cough*.

A cough.

A cough in the middle of a film.

A cough during an adultery scene.

Seemed unnatural to me, artificial.

He caught my eye catching his.

Began to squirm in his master chair in front of the TV.

I witnessed a slow crawl of discomfort gather in his face from its reflection, every time the screen went black.

It moved in the shadowy recesses of his countenance.

Dread.

Doom.

Devastation.

Something awful.

Claustrophobia was beginning to wrap him up like a snake.

Motherfucker could hardly breathe by the time the film was through.

I watched him and felt for him.

Felt sorry for the man.

Guess I wanted to help out.

Lend a hand.

Give him advice.

Cut the cake of wisdom and hand him a slice.

Ah, papa.

Thing is Dad knows I have gifts, powers.

Tries to hide it but he can't deny it.

He knows I can sense things at the drop of a hat and this is why he kind of hates me.

Guess it makes him feel naked, exposed.

Guess it makes the older man seem like the younger one.

The experienced the inexperienced.

Guess it makes him feel like he's under some kind of spotlight, a watchful eye of an all-seeing force.

Something like that.

Whatevs.

He stayed out of my way all week.

Week after that too.

For the rest of the month.

Until the end of time, if he could.

It's no use though, you can't outwait the road which you walk upon.

It just doesn't work like that.

And I am that road.

All roads if I'm being honest with you.

"Dad!"

He was cleaning his motorcycle in the garage when I decided to make my move.

Shed some heavenly light on this situation.

My giant shadow filled up the driveway and made him jump, a little.

"Fucking hell son, don't sneak up on me like that!"

"I did shout you."

"What do you want?" he said, turning his head back to the piece he was polishing.

"I'd like to help out."

"With what?" he said, already irritated.

"I'd like to give you a slice."

He shaded his eyes with his hand.

His mouth looked like a messy squiggle.

"I'm not in the mood for your games," he said.

"I'm offering you a slice."

In that moment I felt myself grow an inch to almost six-foot.

Taller than him, just.

"A slice?"

"Yeah, a slice."

"Of what?"

I took in a deep breath and looked at the clean blue of the sky. "My wisdom."

"What?"

"My wiz."

"What the fuck are you talking about?"

"I know," I whispered, blowing the words across his face.

"Know what?"

"I *always* know, and should know that by now."

Dad lost his metaphorical rag, and then threw his literal one to the floor.

He shouted something and a matchstick paper-boy looked into the garage.

"Bottling it up is no good for the soul. You need to let it out."

"You're starting to wind me up son."

"I know you resent my gifts but you need to understand that I'm using my gifts for the greater good. Ultimately, I'm a highly loving individual."

Dad went to say something else but I touched his wrist. "You're having an affair."

Face drained.

Lips shook.

Fist formed.

His shoes looked silly, especially his laces.

As for me, well I managed to catch myself in the wing-mirror of his motorcycle.

Features so sharp they pricked my own eyes out.

Ouch.

Whoa.

Wow.

The wonder of it all.

This nose.

These teeth.

That jawline.

This chin.

Lethal and angular, like a sexy shark.

I sometimes wonder if I really look like this, or whether God was just taking the piss.

"It's not what you think son," he said, blocking me with the broad of his back.

It's like he was about to talk to the wall.

I watched a house spider dart across the ceiling and disappear into one of the cracks.

He's a part of this moment, I thought – *the spider*.

"It's really not what you think," he said again.

"What do I think?" I said.

He got smaller and his bike got smaller too.

"I don't know," he said a little breathlessly.

I laughed.

"What are you laughing at?" he said with a spray of venom.

"You're saying it's not what I think, but you don't know what I think."

"Don't mock me," he said, boyish whimper this time.

I did a slow three-sixty turn in the garage.

"I don't know what to do son. She won't leave me alone. I keep trying to call it off. But every time I do she threatens to tell your mum, tell everybody. I'm broken, trapped. There's no way out."

"There's always a way out," I said, holding down a yawn.

"I've wanted to come clean to you son but I was afraid you'd never look at me the same again."

"My perception of you hasn't changed Dad. I see you as I've always seen you."

"Thanks," he said, putting his hand on my shoulder in a rare moment of affection. "So," he began. "What shall I do? I must do something."

Finally I took my eyes from my reflection and placed them back on the sky.

A plane crawled across it soundlessly, scratching it with a thin scar of white.

"Do something," I echoed. "Actually I'd do the opposite."

"What do you mean?"

"I'd do nothing."

Exasperation re-twisted his features.

"But she's threatening to tell your mum."

"She won't."

"Why won't she?"

"She just won't."

"But what if she does."

"Then let her."

"What?"

"Let her. In fact tell her to. *Dare* her to."

"Why would I do that?"

"Take her power away."

"But your mum will be heartbroken."

"Doubt it."

"What?"

"Doubt she'll even care."

"Course she will. We've been married for twenty-five years."

"You let sentiment wash you away pops. The real problem with this situation is the noisy manifestations of your own mind."

"What?"

"She won't care. She won't mind. She'll probably just be relieved that you're not bothering her, if you know what I mean."

Dad presented a face of embarrassment, but a spark of recognition flickered in the centre of it.

"There's no need to be crude," he said.

"Do nothing."

"I can't."

"How can you not do nothing? It's the easiest thing to do."
"What?"
"Do less."
"It's not like that."
"Don't do. Don't think."
"Son?"
"The less you do, the more you do."
"I don't even know why I try talking to you son."
"Because I'm in possession of wiz."
"I'm going back inside."
He threw his rag to the floor again and brushed by my shoulder.
"Do less," I shouted up on after him.
He waved me off with an aggressive arm.
"Okay do it your way. Do it the wrong way. Reject my wiz and see where it leads you??" I said. "It's your funeral."

And.

It was.
Is.
I'm here now.
Dad didn't listen.
Dad didn't listen to me.
Don't waste time on guilt, I'd said sometime later.
But.
He did waste time on guilt.
A lot of time.
It ate at him.
Ate him alive.
Ate at him until he was dead.
But it ate at him only when *she* was dead.
Like dying made it worse.
Why do people do that, sentimentalise the dead?
People do act out of proportion around death.
People, glad I'm not one of them.
Anyway I've splashed out on an Armani number for the funeral.
Must say I'm looking hot in the mirror, sunglasses, toothpick.
Fucking Hollywood is what I am.
Roll the toothpick from one corner of my mouth to the other.
I think about Chloe and my heart goes wild.

Just wild.
I'm in love, I decide.
Couldn't really afford the Armani but took out a loan.
Figured the inheritance should even out the cost.
Service kicks off at two.
Had a dentist appointment at ten this morning but had to cancel that bad boy.
Was due a filling and didn't want to wind-up looking like a stroke victim.
Need to be on top-form for the funeral.
Need to be on top-form for Chloe.
She's my baby now.
Hit gym an hour before so my chest and arms look jacked.
Hit rays yesterday and the tan has arrived.
Yep.
I'm ready.
Just like Mama's I get ringside seats.
Which isn't perfect because I can't see who's coming in.
More people than Mam's, all those bitter miners from the 80's.
A church full of black lung and Maggie haters.
Then I see her.
Not the real her but the other her, *Megan.*
Wearing the same AC/DC vest under a black shirt.
Next to her is Aunt Aud and Unc but no Chloe.
No blonde quiff.
My eyes go crazy, hawk-vision over every face in the joint.
Where is she?
How can this be?
The priest fires off but my attention is still on the sea of people and the one missing.
I look at Megan and almost want to scream out loud, *where is she?*
Her face is sad.
And not just funeral-sad.
But at-funeral-without-my-lover sad.
I know how she feels.
This is wrong.
Not right.
Not right at all.
Maybe they've fallen out?

Split up.
Gone separate ways.
For a moment I feel a flash of hope.
But what good is that if I can't get to her?
My brain goes on and before I know it the service is over.
Poems read.
Speeches made.
Ross and Vandross singing over the mourning, moaning people.
Outside I'm ushered into the hearse before I get a chance to ask Megan where my baby is.
Again I pretend I'm in a limousine and again I pretend I'm a movie star.
Only this time it isn't an excitable Matthew McConaughey but a brooding Ryan Gosling.
Throw in a toothpick and stare out the window.
"You alright?" someone says.
I don't answer.
The post funeral party is the same set-up.
Same hall.
Same spread.
Only it is different.
It is different because I *feel* different.
People come up to me only I can't give them what they want.
Not this time.
They stand around, edgy, waiting for me, waiting for me to do something, say something.
The only word I say is, "Megan."
She comes over, head down.
"Sorry for your loss."
"Where's Chloe?"
"She couldn't make it."
"Why?"
"At an audition."
"Audition?"
Nods her head.
"For what?"
"She acts. It's what she does. She's an actor, an actress."
I glance over at the DJ.
Gives me the thumbs-up.
"But she doesn't even talk," I say.

"I know. I don't get it either."
We both look around.
Everyone's eyes are on us, me.
"She should have been here for me," Megan says.
"She should have been here for us *both*."
She looks at me, confused, then sympathy.
"You alright?"
Takes my hands into hers.
"It's hit you hard hasn't it?"
I don't say anything.
Just sit.
I overhear more things from more people.
"See. He *does* care."
"I've never seen him like this."
"So quiet, sullen."
"He put on a brave face at his mum's."

"I guess everyone has their breaking point."

You

This Weirdish Wild Space is placed neatly on the bedside table, while your other arm climbs up the wall and kills the light.

We're all dark now, soft under the covers and together at last. Just, you and I.

"So how was the funeral?" You say.

"Not as enjoyable as the first."

"What?"

I can't believe how warm your skin is, like hot biscuits straight from the oven. I wrap you and rewrap you, so many legs and arms it's like I'm some phenomenal octopus of love. The curve of your back runs down the centre of my torso. This is spooning on a whole new level. A feeling of safety and protection to which you have never known.

"Babe can you not squeeze me to death. I can barely breathe."

"Oh, shit. Sorry. Love-loving just carries me away sometimes."

I make space by putting a paragraph between our supine bodies.

Flip onto my back and lace my fingers across the back of my skull. "Funeral just wasn't the same. Couldn't get into it. Didn't have that vibe."

Sounds like my words have fallen onto a dark sheet of silence so I ask if you are awake.

"Are you awake?"

The bed bows as your body turns and you put your face in front of mine.

"Sorry," You say. "But I really can't concentrate on what you're saying. My mind is still inside the book. His words have tangled me up and I just can't free myself from them. I'm afraid I'm going to have to read some more. One more chapter of *This Weirdish Wild Space* and then I'm all yours, *promise*."

"Is it really *that* good?"

You sigh and your eyes light up in the darkness.

"I believe," You say with an almost intimidated tremor in your voice. "That it could be one of the greatest novels of all-time."

"Okay," I concede, sigh then nod. "If that's the case then you better go."

The hand on my forearm squeezes and you wrinkle your nose in that cute, disarming way.

"Thanks babe. You really are the best."

"I know."

You're up off the bed with the book in your hand. I watch the ghostly outlines of you float towards the bathroom door.

"I'll read in here," You say. "That way I won't disturb you."

Before I know it you are gone, behind the rectangle of wood, framed by yellow light. I hear you on the other side, sitting on the white of the basin, toes touching the cool of the floor, whipping out the bookmark, opening up and starting where you left off; *here* at the top of the 21st page, about to start chapter number **5**, where Our Hero of this novel is telling you that he is now *officially an orphan*.

Girlfriend

Officially an orphan.

    Suppose I should tell my girlfriend.
    She should be back now from Australia.
    We agreed to cut contact while she's gone.
    Hurts too much, she said.
    Of course I agreed.
    Hurts like hell.
    Haven't heard her voice in six months.
    Rock up at her place at noon.
    Knock.
    No answer.
    Ring the bell only I can't hear it.
    So I give the handle a little squeeze.
Hey Presto.
Open sesame.
    I'm in.
    Feel like Tom Cruise as I slip inside; small, sneaky, lithe.
    Nippy little fucker.
    Wearing my usual black.
    If only I had a gun.
    Her rucksack is at the foot of the stairs.
    Not long back, I think.
    Can't wait to surprise her.
    Then I notice another rucksack opposite.
    ?
    Take the stairs by tippy-toe.
    Hear music, maybe something from the 90's.
    Air is thick and moist.
    Steam on glass.
    Door ajar.
    I peer through its crack:
    a duvet-monster with four feet.
    Two of the feet, I recognise.
    The other two, I do not.
    The two I recognise belong to my girlfriend Amber.
    The other two belong to someone else.
    I have not witnessed these feet before.

The duvet-monster is making sounds.
It seems to be enjoying itself so I decide to let it finish.
Float back downstairs and hit the kettle.
Three mugs.
A teabag in each.
Cupboard.
No biscuits.
Damn.
A tray holds the mugs as I drift back upstairs, waiter-style.
Hot beverages hovering over my head.
Through the door.
Towards the bed.
They bolt upright.
Gasp.
Shock.
Fear.
Her face red.
His white.
Mine looks good in the mirror, bit like Colin Farrell.
Or Jude Law with stubble.
"Hope you don't mind my intruding but I've made some tea for us all."
Dude covers himself with the duvet.
Amber covers herself too, but only for a moment.
On recognising me fully she lets it all drop.
"Baby!" she says, a breast plops out.
"My *girl*, back from down-under!"
"Fuck sake didn't I lock the door??"
"How was Oz?"
"Good, amazing. Look – "
"Did you see the wizard?"
"Look let me explain, I'm – "
"At least tell me you brought my boomerang back?"
" – so sorry about this," she says, tearing up a bit, nodding to The Dude on her left.
"G'day mate!" I say brightly.
I introduce myself by handing over his cup of tea.
His mouth wide open.
"I actually kind of fell in love out there," she says with her lip out.
"Hey it happens to the best of us," I shrug a little mournfully,

handing Amber her tea. "I mean you were *out there* for ages. And suppose everyone needs *that love*."

"Does that mean you've cheated on me?"

I sip my tea.

Too hot.

"You ain't gonna believe this girl." I feel Zac Efron come through now; solid, square and smiley. "But I've actually used your absence for abstinence."

"What?"

"At first it was nothing more than an experiment but now it's a whole new way of life. All I can say is that the transformation has been spectacular, *supernatural*. I feel like a new man. In fact *man* feels too underrated a term. What I'm talking about here is more in the realm of the ethereal."

"God I've missed you."

She bounces up on the bed and throws her naked self into my big loving arms.

"I should go," The Dude says, moving slightly.

"Hey man don't be a stranger," I say. "Take a load off. Drink your tea, relax." Amber's face is so close her features blur into a fuzzy pink. "I wanna hear about Oz," I say, "from *both* of you."

"I said *I've missed you*." Amber is now crying some.

"And I've missed *you*."

"No you haven't." She says, bit bitter. "You don't miss anybody."

I look again in the mirror, still Efron.

"I really should go." Dude starts looking around for his clothes.

"Don't. Be. A. Stranger." I say, sing. "You didn't give me your name brother?"

"This is really making me feel uncomfortable."

His face is poised, posed, serious and pointy.

"I tell ya something Amber. He's a good-lookin lad. Fuck. He's *even* better looking than me."

"He's Danish."

"Great Dane!"

"My flight to Copenhagen is in two hours. I should leave."

"Makes sense. Aesthetically superior race, the Scandinavians. It's been proven. *Scientifically*. Second-best looking people after the Ethiopians."

"I really should…"

"I dated a Danish girl once. Spitting imagine of Heather Graham."

"You actually never told me that."

"Or was she Norwegian??"

"I should go."

"You never told me about *her*."

Danish Dude covers himself more while at the same time reaching out for his clothes.

I hook my foot into the hole of his boxer shorts, skilfully lobbing them into the palms of his hands.

"Thanks," he says.

"Finnish your tea."

"I'm sorry for *everything*," he says. "I'm sorry to you *both*."

"Lars stop being so dramatic and finish your tea. Or start it at least."

"My name is not Lars."

"Aw he *is* sweet," Amber says.

"He is," I agree. "And stupidly good-looking but can I just say one thing. Make one minor suggestion. Do you mind making your dialogue a bit more interesting?"

"What?"

"We are currently performing in Joe Cassius' *This Weridish Wild Space* and for me your dialogue isn't up to scratch. It needs sprucing up a bit."

"I'm going," he says, resigned.

He's putting his clothes on now.

"Right now we're in a profound position of privilege, being *in* the 93rd Greatest Novel of All-time and you need to pull your weight, mate."

"Amber, I'm sorry. You never told me he was like this. This, this is too crazy for me."

"That's better Lars," I say, "better dialogue. Using the same word three times is both rhythmic and natural. Natural rhythm."

"My name is not ... look ... I'd like to leave now ... but I ... look ... you're not going to hurt me on the way out, are you?"

"What, hurt you?"

"You're being too fucking cool about this and it's not real and I feel like you're about to be violent."

"Violent?"

"You're acting like a psychopath."

"Hey we're not all like Ted Bundy y'know. Some of us have a heart."

"He's actually not violent," Amber assures, putting her bra back on.

"Truth be told Lars I'm one of the most loving human beings on the face of the planet. Facts. It's been proven, scientifically."

"Fuck."

"I know."

"Look – "

"Look if you want to go Lars, *go*. But I'd much prefer for you to *stay*. Would *love* for you to stay. Take a load off and tell me your name and you can both tell me about Oz and I can tell you about my abstinence and maybe later we can order a takeaway and stick a film on."

Lars is fully dressed by now. "My flight is in two hours."

Funny, there is the sound of a plane overhead at this *exact* moment. Hear it?

"Hey your hair is back to its original red." I say, suddenly to Amber.

"Yup."

"Longer too." I let her hair run through my fingers. "You look like Lindsay Lohan."

"Nah."

"Actually your face is too round for Lohan."

"Thanks for the tea, but I'm going."

"Emma Stone! You look like Emma Stone, dead ringer."

"Aw, thanks baby."

Danish Dude is at the door, still very nervous.

Somehow my physicality shifts into the shape of Dwayne Johnson.

"I need to go, Amber. I'm sorry."

"Sounds like your mind's been made up brother."

He nods, sadly.

"Right, I'm gonna step out of the room for a moment. Make another cup of tea. Give you people some privacy so you can say your goodbyes...your romantic adventure together has been phenomenal, I can tell. I can *feel* it."

Amber and Lars lock and look longingly at each other, the tenderest of moments.

"While I'm out there I'll call you a cab. My treat."

We wave him off to the airport and Lars puts up a slow hand in the rear window.

"I'm gonna miss him."

"Me too," I say.

"Good guy."

"Good looks, tremendous."

"But good *inside*." Amber pleads. "Where it counts."

"Oh yeah, of course." I say. "Naturally."

I can tell by his eye-contact, as he rides out of this scene, that he *almost* gets it.

We watch the cab crawl and climb a distant hill to the cusp of the horizon.

"How come you didn't tell me about the Danish girl?" she says.

"Norwegian."

"And how come you didn't email?"

Amber turns to me, wearing only her underwear.

We are stood next to a cactus plant, on the edge of this blue hour.

"You said not to," I say. "*Hurts too much,* you said."

"Yeah that's what I said but it's not what I *meant.*"

"Oh."

"Don't you know this by now?"

"I guess not. I guess I'm still learning the true language of love."

She smiles and I smile.

"I am sorry about Danish Dude."

I put my head down.

"I'll make it up to you, I promise," she says.

Suddenly a bolt of an idea hits my brain.

"I think I can think of something," I say, casually.

"Oh?"

She puts on a face.

"Double-date," I say.

"What?"

"A double-date."

"A double-date what?"

"Come on a double-date with me."

I notice she has two hands holding onto my one arm.

"With whom?"

"Me, thee, my cousin Megan and her girlfriend, *Chlo*e."

Hairs prick as I hear myself say her name.

27

"Cool." She nods once in a cool pout. "Debt paid. You're easily pleased."

We start to head back inside, away from the sun.

"So has anything happened while I've been away?"

"I became an orphan," I say.

She laughs o' so softly. "Nothing exciting then?"

"Nah, nothing exciting."

You

I remember now, how, we met, you and I. It was all those years ago, remember?

Remember the time I wanted a best friend only I didn't know who to pick. So I sat on a wall at the back of the playground and waited.

Waiting for you, whoever you will be.

Sat in some sort of cosmic trance and waited all day long. There was no rush, but then of course there never has been.

All the kids were running around, either in pairs or groups or by themselves. I watched them all, so many. Playing chase, playing games. All colourful and happy and oblivious. It was like watching a dance, leaves in the wind, random and wayward yet I couldn't help think that there was some kind of design behind it; pattern, rhythm.

I sat still, under the leafy claw of a tree. Half in shade, half in the sun.

No one knew me. No one knew my name. No one knew my face. No one knew I was there.

Then in the opposite corner of the world I saw you for the first time. Couldn't see your face because you had your head down, eyes stuck on your feet as you slowly tightrope-walked a painted line which ran along the edge of the playground. Straight away my mind linked with yours and it was almost as if I was pulling you in, towards me. The journey took forever, a world away, a voyage. Closer and closer you came. It wasn't until you were a metre away that you looked up and saw me, your eyes and my eyes. Startled a little you stepped back.

We looked at each other and something truly amazing happened. A beginning. A birth. The start of a life together.

You silently sat next to me and my view of the playground was shared. We looked at everything before us.

"Don't tell me your name," one of us said.

"I wasn't going to."

"You will always remember this moment."

"I've already forgotten it."

We look around at the children, the school. The trees cut into the blue and white background. We close our eyes and feel the air on our face. The sounds go on all around us, the shouts and screams and the slap of little-feet across the tarmac. Creak of the branch above and the soft hum of traffic in the distance.

"What's it like being a kid again?" I ask.

Your eyes are still closed and you can't quite hear me. You're not really listening.

Days of The Week

MONDAY: Not *again*. I can't handle this.
TUESDAY: Me neither.
WEDNESDAY: We just need to not lose our heads.
THURSDAY: Yes. *Use* our heads, mostly our imagination!
FRIDAY: I'm just so excited right now I can barely breathe.
SATURDAY: Imagine how *I* feel.
SUNDAY: Sorry did somebody say something?
MONDAY: Fuck you I never asked for this.
TUESDAY: No, we didn't.
SATURDAY: Rock n' roll brothers. Rock. And. Fucking. Roll.
SUNDAY: Do you mind keeping it down, one is trying to take a –
MONDAY: Easy for you to say.
TUESDAY: Yeah easy for you.
SUNDAY: Nap.
WEDNESDAY: Fellas, just wait, just, *think* for a moment.
THURSDAY: And *feel.*
FRIDAY: Yes!
THURSDAY: Feel *and* think, create.
MONDAY: Oh this is horrible, this is vile.
TUESDAY: It really is.
MONDAY: The pure drudgery of it all.
TUESDAY: Horrible.
MONDAY: This constant rock on my back.
TUESDAY: This rock and –
SATUDAY: Roll –
SUNDAY: Over. I'm trying to –
SATURDAY: Hey, watch my moves.
SUNDAY: Nap.
FRIDAY: Whoa.
SATURDAY: You like that?
FRIDAY: Wow.
SATURDAY: I like your style too brother.
FRIDAY: But how? I mean wherever did you learn to *move* like that?
SATURDAY: Just, from the block. Just, from around my way.
FRIDAY: I'll be there one day.
SATURDAY: Not a doubt in my mind.
MONDAY: Your complacent position of privilege sickens me.

TUESDAY: Sickens *us*.
WEDNESDAY: It's all about proportion. It's all about balance.
THURSDAY: Knowing where you came from and where you're going.
WEDNESDAY: The middle ground. The straight road.
THURSDAY: Gutters and stars.
WEDNESDAY: The means between the extremes.
THURSDAY: Roots and clouds.
MONDAY: Clouds don't have roots, idiots.
TUESDAY: Fools.
FRIDAY: All this talk is making me want to blow. I'm on the edge.
SATURDAY: Just let it all out, brother.
MONDAY: And *you*.
SATURDAY: Me?
MONDAY: Yes, you.
SATURDAY: What about me?
MONDAY: All show and surface.
TUESDAY: Shallow.
MONDAY: All style and no substance.
TUESDAY: None.
SATURDAY: Hair down and painting the town –
MONDAY: Gone.
TUESDAY: Done.
SATURDAY: That's me.
MONDAY: That's you.
SATURDAY: Does what it says on the tin.
MONDAY: Gone before I know it.
TUESDAY: Before *we* know it.
SATURDAY: Baby.
MONDAY: User.
WEDNESDAY: Okay calm down.
MONDAY: Bastard.
TUESDAY: Bastards, the lot of you.
MONDAY: Wouldn't last a day in my shoes.
TUESDAY: Our shoes.
WEDNESDAY: We are all needed and necessary.
THURSDAY: For the tension and release.
WEDNESDAY: We all serve a purpose.
THURSDAY: For the parts of the whole.
MONDAY: There's a hole in mine but nobody understands.

TUESDAY: I do, *I* understand.
MONDAY: Hardly.
TUESDAY: But I hang on every word you say.
WEDNESDAY: You can't stay in the dark forever, my friend.
THURSDAY: It's getting brighter every day.
FRIDAY: But tomorrow never comes. I've been waiting my *entire* life.
SATURDAY: Tomorrow is *now.*
SUNDAY: Did somebody say something?
MONDAY: Oh no not you again.

Letter

Amber went nuts when she found out that I had *actually* become an orphan while she was away. I mean *totally* lost her fucking mind. Just deranged. Amber turned red. When she finally stopped whaling she said.

"How can you actually joke about this?"

"When did I joke about this?"

"You said, *I became an orphan.*"

"I did because I have."

"You're sick."

"You're the one who brought the joke to it. I just told you the facts."

"You're actually not normal. I loved your mum and dad. They were like parents to me."

"Do you want a hug?"

"I want you to leave me alone."

"Are you just saying this or do you *mean* it."

She was gone.

Two days later I received a letter from her.

I'm writing to you becarse you don't beleeve in emails and u didnt email me while I was away and u don't beleeve in emails and you don't beleeve in anything and you don't believe in life and you don't beleeve in death and I carnt have this in my life rite now or ill die not now or not ever!!!!

Girl needs to Full Stop. Or at least comma, once in a while. Something to tell you about Amber. She's been diagnosed with both dyslexia and bipolar. She's also on the autism spectrum and she's been diagnosed with ADHD.

I no you have a personality disorder or emotional disorder (witch you still wont get diagnosed but this is ACTUALLY draning the dead life out of me u didn't think too tell me that an horrifc thing like this could happen while I was away its just awful and unatural and just severely severely <u>wrong!!!</u> Four days I was back in the cuntry before I find this out and I have to find out by janet from the shop how does that make me look and feel. Maybe lars was rite you are a freak I feel *in love with you becarse you are that bit different but to not even tell me or show no feeling like its casual like you have forgotten to by milk or something from the shop I mean WTF I cant be around you I need space I am still grieving and morning myself and the shock is just to much rite now so leeve me be and Ill be in contact you perhaps in the very distent furute but I ACTUALLY feel like all my foundations are crumbling and there is noon to catch me any moor and austarlia was suppose to make me better but now things are just tentimes as worse than b4. I should have typed this letter for the speeling check but the printer is broke and u needed to get this letter <u>quick</u> !!! and my dyslexia is allways worse when Im in the manic faze of my bipolar but youll just have to make the best of this letter and reed between its lines maybe your ACTUALLY burying this shit in deep inside and that's why ur pretending to not care the familee is in bits if you didn't notice yet u swan around in your new suits well Im just rambling now contct me if you need but my guess is you wont.*

See you around.

Amber

Didn't understand a word of that, did you? But my guess is she was pissed. Which is not good. Not good at all. My double-date. I had to find somebody else.

Double-date

So.

I pick you up in my new soft-top.
Beep, beep.
Living room window frames you.
You shake your head through the glass and leave the house.
Door.
Shut.
Lock up.
Walk your driveway.
Haven't seen me in years.
"Since when did you drive?" You say.
I don't answer.
Just remove my shades.
Eyes.
You look into them.
Then at the curves in my car.
"Take it you've gone up the career ladder."
"Down," I say.
"How do you afford this bad boy then?"
"Step inside," I say.
You do.
"Haven't seen you in years," You say.
"Years," I say.
We drive.
I drive you.
Scenic route.
Country lanes.
"So what is this double date?" You say.
"Nothing really. Just catching up with my cousin and her girlfriend."
"And your cousin is a girl?"
"She is."
You are mystified but happy to see me.
Be with me again.
You are back.
We are back.
You and I.

The force, the unit.
Back from the old times, back from the classroom.
I appreciate this.
Helping me out this way.
Coming to the rescue.
Without you I'd have no one.
And.
I wouldn't get to see her.
It's that weird feeling again.
That feeling I've never felt before.
Nerves.
I need a piss, a shit.
Hands wet at the wheel.
Dry mouth.

"Megan is cool." I say. "You'll like her. She's a bit Gothy and dark but she's a laugh."

"And her girlfriend?"

I hope you don't notice my nerves.
My intensity.
My obscurity.
My love.
My desire.
The burning from within.
Abracadabra.

"Chloe," I cough. "She's quiet. I don't think she even talks. She's an actor, an actress. I've only met her once."

Still you are mystified.
But so, so happy to be with me.
By my side.
I open the car door for you and we head towards the restaurant.
Open this door for you, too.
I don't feel like any movie star tonight and this is not good.
Try and force DiCaprio but he doesn't arrive.
Luckily we're here first.
Before them.
I pull out the chair for you and we sit, opposite.
Please Chloe sit across from me so I can see you.
Please Chloe sit next to me so I can touch you.

"You alright?" You say.

"Yeah. Why?"

"You don't seem the same."
You're the same.
Notice what others miss.
You make me vulnerable.
You make me valuable.
You make me strong.
You push me to my limits.
Take me to my edge.
I wouldn't want anyone else with me on a night like this.
So glad it's you and not Amber.
So glad she bailed.
"I'm good," I say.
Again we share *that look*.
I see Megan.
Her lesbian walk past the window.
I'm literally on fire, alive, feels fucking amazing, this rush.
She stops.
Mimes to someone out of picture.
Mouths, *come on*.
Enters restaurant.

Seconds later another figure moves past the window, blonde flick.

That blonde flick.
Song *Hungry Eyes* plays in the restaurant.
Yours have been on me the whole time.
You seem to know that this night *means something*.
A coming together of forces.

I stare at a jar of mustard for about five seconds before my eyes drift.

Up.
Megan.
Big, butch and beaming.
Chloe.
Behind.
She floats just like I do, without sound.
Eyes at the floor.
Unsmiling.
Then.
Blonde flick.
Looks at me.

Then at you.

The four of us are here.

Swayze

I've worked out that life hasn't been the same since Patrick Swayze died. The world is that bit different, now he is gone. Not quite the same. He's left a gap in all of us, I think, whether we like to admit it or not. I see it in people's faces sometimes, *ah, Swayze*. I mean who could not be moved by such emotional masterpieces as *Dirty Dancing* and *Ghost*. He was always making us cry. Always taking us to the next level. Always putting himself on the line. Always putting others before him. There was something sacrificial in his performances. Like a deer trapped in headlights. Like he knew he wasn't perfect but was willing to die for the cause. I wouldn't say he was the greatest actor. I wouldn't even say he was the most charismatic actor. But what he was, was, a *loving* actor. Maybe the most loving actor of all-time. He was protective, not just to his female lead but also to the audience at home, *us*. I mean you could really *feel* that he was on your side. That he really cared. It just oozed from the man. His depth was incredible, undeniable. Even though he was a part of Hollywood he never got lost in all that. He was once quoted saying: "Good-looking people turn me off. Myself included." To have this kind of vision and self-knowledge is breath-taking. What he also had, which others did not, was this warm interchangeability, in that he could quite easily be the cuddler or the cuddleree. He was strong and fragile at the same time. He needed us as much as we him. In short, he was a real hero, a real human being. And there really was no end to the man's talents. He could act, dance. Even sing. *She's Like The Wind*. I mean WTF! Have you ever heard anything like it? What a fucking song. *I look in the mirror, and all I see, is a young old man, with only a dream...she's out of my league...just a fool to believe...she's like the wind.* The song aches. It *pines*. It physically hurts. Such heroic vulnerability, masculine tenderness. Ah. Gets me every time. Everyfuckingtime. Yep. Life hasn't been the same since. The world is that bit different, now he is gone. That bouncy walk and the shake of his head. His laugh. His pain. His innocent blue eyes. His heart. His soul.

Miss that guy.

You

You put this book down and smile and shake your head and almost laugh out-loud cos you know what he means about Swayze cos you've often thought the same. In fact most of the things in *This Weirdish Wild Space* you get. You get it cos you get me and that's what I truly love about you. Your head, your brain. No one has ever been able to pin your mind down and that's what I love. You don't think like the rest and you never have. You take in what others miss. You are so, *so* observant, almost to the point of a sub-human level. And the fact you don't feel the need to talk about it makes it even more mind-blowing. Your mind just roams on through the ages, free and limitless, awesome and astral. It really is like your mind is *all* minds. Like there is just one, universal mind and you so get that.

This is why I love you and need you around. This is why I need you to keep reading this book. I need you to keep reading this book because you *are* this book. You are at the very core of its chaos and that is just so damn crucial. So damn beautiful. You are the writer, the reader, and the muse, ALL rolled into one.

I mean, how insane is that?!

Whoa.

Apple Tree Lane

Amber spoke to me, at last.

"I want my things back."
"Things?"
"Photography books. CD's. Stuff. Things."
"Oh. Sure. Come get them."
"I'm working lots. You don't work at all. Thought maybe you could ACTUALLY drop them round. Considering…"
"Oh. Sure."
Long pause.
"I do love you…you know?" I say.
"Mm."
Silence.
Ice cream van in the background.
"I need time," she says. "One day we can be friends."
When the call is over I go in search of her things.
There are more things than I expect.
It fills a suitcase.
I carry it across town.
Then onto a bus.
At her house I find the key in a plant pot and let myself into the shed.
Lay the suitcase down.
Look around.
Loads of bugs n' flies.
Spider weaving a webby kingdom in the corner.
Throw a few bugs in but the spider won't take the bait.
It's like she knows I'm here.
On the way back I stop off at a coffee shop for a pot of tea.
"Do you have biscuits?"
"Sorry?" she says.
"Do you *sell* biscuits?"
She is looking directly at my forehead.
"We have muffins and flapjacks."
"Nah, not the same." I say.
I sit and sip and look at the people.
Their faces.
Eyes.

Mouths.
The way they talk and flirt and pretend.
After I skip the bus and decide to walk all the way home.
Maybe five or six miles.
Seven, even.
It's a nice day.
Sun.
Breeze.
Birds.
Apple Tree Lane.
I walk up it backwards, looking at the church.
At the top there's a woman standing at her garden gate.
Old.
Very old.
60, 70 or 80.
Never been good at ages.
I'm even worse with kids.
I wouldn't know if a kid was 2 or 4 or 7.
Seriously.
The old woman is thin and flaky and so, so tanned.
Nipples stick through her vest.
Her eyes are funny, like she is cross-eyed, or even blind.
"Michael is that you?" she says.
Looking right at me.
Blind, I think.
"Son," she says.
Yelp of desperation in her voice, *son*.
"Yes," I say.
"Oh son you're late."
"By how long?"
"I don't quite know."
We stare at each other.
"Well come in from the cold," she says, sun in her eyes.
"Okay then."
"Dinner is served."
She turns and walks back into the house.
Her skirt is thin.
See her knickers.
Inside her house.
Nothing out of place.

Like my joint, minus the dust.
I write my name in it.
Follow her through to the kitchen.
Wooden spoon.
Stirs a big pot of stew.
Steam.
Smells like a dream, heaven.
Serves up.
Can't be blind.
Must be dementia.
Delusion.
Loneliness.
We sit, trays on lap.
Watch her bones move as she eats.
She's so small.
Fragile.
Blow her over.
Snap her with my fingers.
I study every inch of her.
Every vein.
Every mole.
One kneecap doesn't look real.
"Enjoying that son?"
"Delicious," I say.
"Good. Keep going. Don't stop."
"Need toilet."
"You know where it is."
"I do."
I don't.
Walk the house.
Stair-lift.
Cords dangling everywhere.
Doorstopper that looks like an anvil.
Toilet.
Piss.
Shake.
Flush.
On sitting back down I notice a photo.
Her a few years back with a big fat boy.
That's me, I think.

Supposed to be me.
Me in this moment.
Me in her maybe-blind eyes.
Me in her mind.
He is I.
His spirit inhabits my body.
I feel a bond with this big fat boy.
We're the same, somehow.
"Will you get that kitchen knife?" she asks.
"What for?"
"Cut up the cake."
I do.
Slice the lemon cake into six.
In the reflection of the blade I look a bit like Christian Bale.
We eat the cake and then lie back.
Her nipples are now really sticking through her vest, twice the size as before.
She points the remote at the TV and fires it up.
Takes my hand and we watch the 1953 film, *Shane*.
She dozes off.
Then.
I doze off.
When we wake we're still holding hands and the credits roll to the end of the film.
String of saliva swings from her bottom lip.
She wipes it off and looks up at me.
"I had a dream."
"What happened?"
She looks slightly scared, like she has just realised the truth.
You're not my son Michael.
"I don't remember," she says, at last.
We sit until she is properly awake.
"Son."
"Mum."
"Go to that cupboard and open the bottom drawer."
I do as I'm told.
There are four stacks of twenty pound notes.
"Take one," she says.
My thumb rips down the corner of each stack.
Wow.

"Take one son. Treat yourself."
I look at her, sat there.
Close the drawer.
"Nah. I'm good."
"But you haven't got a job. You're not working."
"I know. But I don't need money right now. I have enough."
"Stubborn. Just like your old man," she says.
At the gate.
She says goodbye.
Hugs me.
Holds me.
Kisses me on the head.
The cheek.

Lips.

You

When you are ill I will carry you to bed and wrap you up for days, until you are better. Make a gentle place for you. Duvet, blankets, and pillows. Lay beside you, whisper, rock you to sleep and back. I will take the chaos from your head and tell you that *everything is alright*. Because, it is. I will go away if you want me to, but never too far. Go and come back. Let in the sun and keep out the cold. Bring you whatever you need, magazines, fruit. Soup, water. Soothing music. Talk to you until your head unravels and you are clear again. Paint stars on your ceiling. Read you stories. Take you to places you've never been. A faraway land where the weather is warm. Hour by hour you'll get better. Feed you love. Make you laugh, giggle. Stroke your back and blow on your eyes. Fingers through hair. Massage everywhere; toes, feet, legs, back, arms, hands, fingers, neck, head, scalp, face. Place my palm over your tum and take away the ache and sickness. Keep you cool. Keep you warm. Make things simple again. Take away the noise and the mess and the sharp edges. I'll show you the way. Lead the way. Tell you how it all works. How to breathe into it and be free. Nothing will escape my attention. I will be everywhere, and nowhere, for you.

Chloe

I now know what I want from her.

    What I need from her.
    I now know what she means to me and what I have to do.
    Calf.
    Chloe's calf.
    I need for her to allow me to touch her calf, love her calf.
    Really.
    It means everything.
    I love her and I'm in love with her and this experience will embody it all.
    It makes sense.
    It makes sense to *me*.
    I have my mission, my destiny.
    And so.
    The restaurant worked that night.
    Dinner was a whirling dream.
    Time played tricks.
    It slowed down and sped up at different points.
    Some of it I remember, in microscopic detail.
    The rest is blank.
    I don't recall what any of us ate, or drank.
    But I remember the green specks in Chloe's eyes and the moles on her neck.
    We became two worlds on one table.
    Something was happening between you and Megan.
    You two, just, clicked.
    Talk.
    Laughter.
    Noise.
    Your energy was overwhelming.
    At one point I thought you were going to start dancing.
    Chloe and I were opposite.
    We were silent.
    Her silence made me silent.
    Peace.
    Softness.
    Slowness.

She looked at me, sometimes.
Head down.
Eyes up.
Unbeatable blue.
Dark rings around them.
Sapphire in shadows.
Resting upon me.
Into me.
Through me.
Fearless.
Not confrontational.
Not even *penetrating*.
But deep.
Deeper.
Deepest.
Then she'd look away, to the side, at Megan.
Blonde flick.
Back to her food.
Window.
Ceiling.
Back at me, again.
There is a whole new language in her face.
I couldn't stop looking at her.
Guess you could say I was captivated.
Perplexed.
Hypnotized.
Taken.
I have never been *taken* before.
You and Megan carried on, oblivious of us as we were of you.
"Who's your favourite serial killer?" one of you said.
"For all-round dynamism and sophistication I'd have to go with Bundy. But for pure passion and rock star quality Ramirez wins every time."
"You can't beat Shipman's work-rate though. Boy was prolific."
"Not a true serial killer though. Bit of a pussy. I mean he wasn't *hands on* was he?"
"True."
You both thought this was hilarious.
I rolled my eyes at Chloe.
Dark humour.

I just don't get it.
As if the world isn't cruel enough.
It's when we stood I saw it for the first time.
Emerging from her long skirt as she walked away from the table.
It was the most beautiful thing I'd ever seen.
Chloe's calf.
Right calf.
So white and perfect.
A dove.
A piece of fruit.
A porcelain heart.
I had to touch it.
It was my place.
In the car park it was as if we were going to leave this way.
You and Megan in one car.
Us in the other.
Chloe looked right at me.
She knew.
Knew she had complete power over me even though I had power over everybody else.
The surrender was exhilarating.
I'm sure she said something, handful of small words.
Sounded like, *this is it*.
I could have imagined this.
Like some audio hallucination.
Megan was laughing when she got in the car.
Chloe followed.
One leg.
Then the other.
Left.
Then right.
I watched *it* disappear.
You and I waved them off.

The sun and moon were out at the same time.

You

"Still reading that book?" I say.

"I am," You say.

You have it in your hands and I see your smile hovering over the cover. Only you seem freer with it now, more relaxed, less intense. It's like you're taking your time, eating up the words carefully; one by one, like grapes.

"What's it about anyway?" I say.

The rest of your face is here as you lower the book into your lap. A cute question mark wriggles into your expression as you think.

"Hm. Hard to explain. It's kind of a love story."

I sit next to you on the grass and look up the hill. A guy and a girl are walking down it hand-in-hand.

"I'll have to lend it to you once I'm through," You say.

"Nah," I say. "You know I'm not much of a reader."

For some reason I am suddenly filled with a horrible flood of self-doubt. Like I'm not good enough for you, not clever enough. Wish I read. Wish I'd paid more attention at school.

The couple from the hill walk by us only you don't notice them, too busy thinking about *This Weirdish Wild Space*. The couple, both the boy and the girl, look down at me.

First I'm taken aback by how handsome the guy is, like some kind of movie star. His girlfriend seems out of place next to him; plain, pale, miserable. I watch her boyish calf muscle flex before my eyes. *Gross,* I think.

"Alright?" the guy nods.

"Alright," I reply, clearly intimidated by his dangerous looks.

Girl says nothing.

You haven't even noticed them as they walk on by.

"The book is kind of funny. Like you can't work out if it's supposed to be a comedy or not. The main character is an idiot though. I hate him. I hate him but I'm kind of in love with him too. He's like this super-arrogant guy yet you can't help but adore the fact that he doesn't take anything seriously. To be honest the main character kind of reminds me of you."

I pull up a small clump of grass from the earth and the scratching sound sounds like Velcro.

"You think I'm arrogant?" I say, hurt.

"What? No. I mean … there's *parts* of the main character that reminds me of you."

I look up and the couple are now stick-figures on the horizon. I can just make out the girl's quiff bouncing as she walks.

"What's his name?" I say with a sigh.

The book is covering your face again. *This Weirdish Wild Space* is staring right at me.

"Y'know," You say. "I don't know. I don't even think Joe Cassius gave him a name."

Joe Cassius. It bugs me that you talk about him like you know him. Like he's a real person in Real Life. Kind of pathetic, I think.

I look over and the couple are now gone, as if they never existed.

Her Printer is Actually Fixed Now

Letterbox. Clap. Envelope. Amber's handwriting.

I get a paper cut on my thumb as I open it.

To You,

As you can see my printer is ACTUALLY fixed now so you don't get to suffer my handwriting and spelling although I don't get why you don't use emails in the first place because it's ten times easier. Anyway. I'm calm now and feeling better and my meds are working and we get to have a civilised conversation instead of me rambling on like some retarded madwoman. I think another reason that I'm feeling better is because I can't believe it but I've ACTUALLY met someone and this is the real reason I'm writing to you. And know this isn't to get you jealous although you don't do jealousy or any emotion really but I thought I'd just give you an update on my life seeing as though we were together for like four years. Gosh. I hate writing. Even with the spell check and stuff and still find this hard because of my dyslexia and words have always been tricky and tripped me up although you'd never think so because I'm such a great talker. If only we could communicate in pictures and oh another thing my photography has been accepted at this exhibition in London and she said I could be like the next Diane Arbus so as you can see I have turned my life around. Ben is wonderful. No offense but he is the very opposite of you in everyway. He ACTUALLY feels a lot. And he does get kind of jealous and a little possessive and I ACTUALLY like that because I'm not used to it and it shows he cares. I always used to call you doctor cool but really it should have been doctor cold because that's how you were at times but you know what I really am 100% over you now and I won't even start talking about your mum and dad cos I really will just burst into total tears. There. Another thig amazing with Ben is that he just has loads of friends and he's always out and taking me out and you're just always on your own and you never do nothing but go wondering around at night on your own I mean what is that. Any way I do still care about you and I'm sure we'll be ok eventually. You have had a power of me for such a long time and you should be glad that I've met the man of my dreams. So maybe you should leave me be for a while so me and ben can get too know each other. Thanks for bringing my stuff back and putting it in the shed that was really good of you and you are a good person inside even though no one really gets to see it in fact no one rarely gets to see anything but that's ok because that's just you.

Take care and get an email address so we can ACTUALLY communicate.

A X

Night Out

She's right.

    He does like to go out at night.
    Take to the streets.
    Go where *they're* not.
    Walk around.
    Wander.
    See what he can find.
    Black.
    He wears all black.
    Trainers.
    Socks.
    Pants.
    Jeans.
    Vest.
    T-shirt.
    Sweater.
    Coat.
    Hat.
    Gloves if it's cold.
    He likes it out here.
    Feels pure.
    Primitive.
    Raw.
    The truth.
    The night is never dull.
    Always spectacular.
    Awesome.
    A mystery.
    It wraps him up and gives him power.
    Like the AC/DC song, *Night Prowler*.
    Ah.
    Bliss.
    Alone with the world.
    Like it's all his.
    He can do what he wants with it.
    Visit people.
    People he knows and people he doesn't know.

Swing by.
Drop in.
Watch over while they sleep.
He puts his ear to the wall and imagines what *they're* doing.
Sleeping.
Fucking.
Watching TV.
Thinking about me.
Him.
The hero of this novel.
The anti-hero of this book.
He keeps getting this real powerful feeling though.
Every time he passes this certain house by the park.
Turquoise.
Brown door.
Hanging baskets either side.
Black cat on the fence.
Feel Chloe.
Little window at the back.
Puts his fingers on the glass, *baby.*
She's asleep on the other side, he knows.
Or just lying there.
On her back.
Staring at the dark.
She doesn't sleep much at all.
If ever.
Hence the dark rings.
From there.
He takes her with him.
Takes her into the fields.
They walk.
Talks to her in his head.
Of course she never talks back but she's *here.*
In the fields there's a billion stars.
All over him like a rash.
It's glorious.
He sits in the grass and stares at the cows.
They stare back.
White in the night.
Black cows.

Don't know they're here until their breath is on his face.
Black and white cows.
Look weird, like different cow-parts floating mid-air.
When he can't sleep he imagines he's out wandering.
When he's out wandering he imagines he's tucked up in bed.
Sometimes he loses track of where he is and his body disappears and it's just his mind.
Like he's in two places at once.
Inside *and* outside.
He goes out when he feels like it.
Not every night.
Not even every week.
Months may pass.
But at some point he'll be out.
After dark.
Somewhere.
Out.

Here

Alec Baldwin

I met Alec Baldwin in New York City. It was the January before the towers got hit. I was walking through Central Park in the snow when I saw some commotion way off in the yonder, by a bridge. On the bridge people were overlooking a film set. The director's chair said, "Alec Baldwin." I saw this as a coincidence because people had been telling me I looked like Alec Baldwin my whole life. He looked cool, shading his eyes, observing a plane that was passing overhead.

"Cut," he shouted, annoyed. "God damn plane."

A black guy next to me got really excited because Jennifer Love Hewitt was there but I didn't know who she was. After the scene was shot I went on down to meet him. Everyone thought I was insane but I didn't see what all the fuss was.

"Alright Al."

Security tried to stop me but Alec waved them off. Fucker was tall. And *stupidly* handsome.

"People say you look like me."

"Is that right?" he said, laughing a little.

He looked at me and I looked at him.

"Did you want an autograph?"

"Autograph," I said. "Why would I want an autograph?"

He laughed again. "I dunno."

"I just wanted you to meet me."

"Okay then."

He shook my hand, and left.

You

You don't know you're doing it. You don't know you're doing it and if you did there would be no point. Defeats the whole object. You might think you know but trust me there's a level even under *that*. You don't know you're doing it and because of this you blame all the reasons under the sun. There are eight million of you on the earth at one time, moving without sound. You are one of them. If you meet another one you cancel each other out. Bump heads for a second and then move in the opposite direction. Onto someone else. The only way to know you is behind the eyes. Behind the eyes because there is nothing there. If we were to cut you open something green would crawl out. An alien or a lizard or another reptile. Serpent. A single mosquito whirring through the hottest night of the year.

You haven't got a clue what I'm talking about, have you?

Daylight Robbery

There was a smack of something in the mouth.

Stark daylight in my eyes, and stars.
When I came to I was pushed up to a wall with blood in my mouth and a knife pointing right at me, at my stomach.
One hooded figure held me strong and immovable while the other hooded figure did all the talking.
"Make any noise and *this* goes right in you."
Next to me was the illuminated square of an ATM.
Tuesday-afternoon-people walked casual and unawares in the daylight.
The tip of the blade was now placed perfectly into the hole of my bellybutton.
Suddenly I get a flashback, or more accurately, a *flash-forward*, if there is such a thing.
Almost a premonition although I don't really know what this means.
And the present has more pressing matters to attend to.
The man holding me is big, supernaturally strong and the smell emitting from his breath ain't great.
The man doing the talking bears a striking resemblance to a thuggish Daniel Craig, a dead ringer.
"Has anyone ever told you you look like – "
"Shut-the-fuck-up."
The man holding applies more pressure to my arms and I wince a bit.
"Now get that wallet out man, nice and easy."
I try but both arms won't move.
"Sorry old chap, but the physics of this situation won't allow it."
"What?"
Daniel Craig has a downwards scar lining his face that looks kind of cool, really enhances his brooding scowl. He nods at Breath Boy and he loosens his grip.
"Thank You," I say. "Now what can I do for you boys?"
"Money."
"Oh sure, how much would you like?"
"How much can you draw in one go?" Daniel Craig says, he's getting nervous, starts looking around.

"As street-robbing entrepreneurs, you should really know this information."

"I don't like your fucking lip."

I feel my lip starting to pulse and swell, the sharpness in my bellybutton increases as Craig pushes in a little more.

"Alright," I wince. "I get the point."

"Try two-hundred," he says.

"You know," I say. "I seem to think it's three."

"Three-hundred?"

"Yes."

"Well fucking try that then."

Breathy lets me turn and extract my wallet, the thin blue line of Barclays is whipped-out and away we go.

I see our dark reflection in the screen of the ATM:

A handsome face between two hooded figures.

I think of Tom Cruise in the film *Eyes Wide Shut*.

"You know this is kind of like a movie," I say. "Kind of exciting, this is the first time I've ever been robbed."

"Say one more word and it'll be your last."

What a line!

The blade is now sharp at my back, my side, in the kidney area, I think.

I have the money and now they have the money.

They both look happy now.

"So what is it lads, drugs?"

"Shut-the-fuck-up."

"Wanna go and grab a coffee somewhere, a pot of tea, talk about it? My treat."

"What?"

"Maybe I can supply you with Wiz."

"You carrying some?" Daniel says, his eyes big.

"Oh no," I laugh. "Whiz without the H. Wiz. I can supply you with my wisdom."

"Shut-the-fuck-up and give me your phone."

I put my hand in my pocket for a moment, think.

"Ah lads," I say. "Can we skip this part?"

"What?"

"The money I don't mind cos I'll get all that back on insurance but the phone is a total hassle, all those numbers and the rigmarole of getting set up with a new one. Could we *please* skip this part.

Haven't I been the model victim, a shining example of benevolence and good-humoured willingness. Plus, people are starting to look over. It is broad daylight after all. You boys should really start thinking of working the Night Shift. Although this hiding-in-plain-sight method seems to be working out for you so far. "

Daniel Craig looks confused and Breath Boy speaks for the first time. "He's got a point."

The knife looks at me and even *he* seems to agree.

"Okay," Craig concedes at last. "Just don't go calling the feds straight away. Give us time to get away first."

"Thank You for understanding about the phone thing, and yes, your wish is my command." I nod, graciously.

"Cheers mate," one of them says.

"Yeah, cheers," the other one adds.

"No thank *you*. I'll take all the adrenalin and literary inspiration I can get these days."

They nod, look around a bit, nod again.

And then they are gone.

I watch the little scallywags pace fast and hard into the crowds, until they blend in, until they are like everybody else.

You

We'd not long met and already I was stroking your hair without thinking about it, like it was the most natural thing in the world, like maybe I'd known you for a decade, or half a decade at least.

"I like that," You said.

"I know," I said.

I was surprised by your place. Maybe even blown away. It was in the middle of the forest, surrounded by pine trees and nature was all around us. I liked hanging out there in the day while you went to work. I enjoyed washing your dishes and tidying the place up. Not OCD tidy but just the right amount. Then I'd go on big long walks down wild roads which lead to nowhere. You told me to watch out for rattlesnakes and trucks and crazy farmers with big guns but it was the cows which scared me most. They were bigger than European cows and more pissed off. They hunted me down and I had to hide behind rocks and wait for them to go. By the time the walk was over had I blisters on my feet and cramp in my shoulder but I didn't care cos I knew you were on your way home by now.

And in the evenings we would go out to the Korean restaurant or stay in and watch Patrick Swayze movies.

"Miss that guy."

"Me too."

Couldn't Quite Get Our Eyes to Meet

Last time I saw Amber was on my Mum's birthday.

    Although I didn't know at the time.
Maybe I had forgotten.
I don't remember.
We had just finished working on Amber's memoir, *A Picture in Words: a photographer's battle with dyslexia.*
"I'm happy with this, so far," she said, laughing a little.
I looked at a photo of her as a baby and agreed.
We left the house at noon and walked through the park until we were stopped by a dead squirrel.
Lying on the pavement, sideways like a fish.
"Is that actually what death looks like?" she said.
"His teeth are freaky."
"How do you know he's a he?"
"I don't."
We left her there and walked on, over the cobbles, past the castle.
The city looks different every time.
Last night was a late one.
We ate a big Korean feast and then watched both the *Poltergeist* films.
New one at the cinema and the old one in bed.
The old one was better.
They always are.
It was 2pm the following day when I got really fucking hungry.
"I'm fucking starving."
"Me too," she said.
We looked out for restaurants.
Finally choosing this American-style diner that was near her old office.
She walked up to the window, looked through.
"There's my old desk, old chair, old kettle."
In the restaurant this toothy fuck ambushed us at the door. "Hi guys!"
He was cradling two menus like it was a baby.
We followed him to a table.
While he fetched our drinks Amber said, "I don't trust him one bit."

"Me neither. But we've got to eat, soon, fast, *now*."

"Okay."

The tables were wooden and I imagined splinters in my food but I was so hungry I didn't care.

I had chicken drenched in barbeque sauce and she had something healthier.

I liked it all, in the end.

Amber said she would never come back here again, *ever*.

I paid up and went for a piss and when I returned she was gone.

I started looking around.

"Alright sir?" It was Toothy Fuck.

"I seemed to have lost my GF."

"GF?"

I thought everybody knew what GF meant these days and I couldn't be bothered to explain.

At last she appeared.

World was better now we were full.

We were back on the streets, walking around.

"I forgot to take my vitamins."

"And I could do with a nap."

By Lloyds Bank we talked about arguments and how they were kind of pointless because in five years' time nobody will remember a thing.

Crossed the zebra.

Hit the shops.

Amber looked at clothes for a long time because that's what she likes to do.

I looked around at the people and tried to work out which ones were real.

She bought something, I think.

Don't quite remember.

So on Kings/Queens Street we parted ways.

Our afternoon together was over.

I got on the bus and sat at the back.

Looked at her through the window and she was looking back but we couldn't quite get our eyes to meet.

Her Second Film

"I need some gum."

If you want to see what Chloe looks like in Real Life then you should go and see this movie she's in. It's her second film, I think. She plays the part of a 17-year-old girl that has an affair with a middle-aged alcoholic, Tommy.

You first see her at a funeral. Tommy is kneeling at the coffin, paying his respects. He starts to sway from side to side and you realise he's fallen asleep. She enters the shot from his right, kneels beside him. It's Chloe as you know her. Flicks her quiff, dark eyes. She doesn't talk. Looks at Tommy, then away again. She's on screen for no longer than half a minute, then gone.

"I need some gum."

Those are the first words you ever hear from her. *I need some gum.* It's not how you expected her voice to be. Maybe it is. You don't know. It's kind of deep, but soft. Tommy has inherited an ice cream truck from the dead man. Only he is terrible with kids. A lousy ice cream man. She jumps up the truck, scares Tommy.

"I need some gum."

She takes some and chews it. Wears a stripy top and cut-off jeans. Has her leg up, showing the calf. She pretends she is 14 but really she is 17. Flirts with him. Tommy doesn't quite know how to deal with her. Her dad then catches them, mid-flirt. He comes up to the truck.

"Tommy, whatcha doin?"

He is big and powerful. He is Tommy's ex brother-in-law, Jerry. He invites Tommy in for dinner. The four of them sit around a table, Jerry, Jerry's wife, Tommy, and Chloe. Tommy and Chloe sit facing. Silently looking at each other. Chloe doesn't eat meat although she doesn't want to be called a vegetarian. She starts talking about how chickens peck each other's eyes out and Jerry gets mad and crashes his fist down on the table.

"Don't talk like that at the table!"

She starts hanging-out at the ice cream truck with Tommy, more and more.

"I had a dream about you last night."

She wears a pink crop-top. You can see her stomach. She moves the quiff just like in Real Life only her smile is different. She keeps talking and you can't quite piece it all together.

"You know her?"

She acts jealous. She has no name. She goes to a bar even though she's underage.

"I'm old enough. Ask my boyfriend."

Tommy gets in trouble. They get thrown out the bar. They go back to a house party. She wears an earring with a little silver chain that connects the top of her ear to the bottom. Has a little make-up on too. Her skin looks tan. She smokes pot without inhaling. Tommy tries to get her up to dance but she won't. Instead she sits on a wooden chair while he dances around her foolishly. She laughs, bouncing her knees up and down real fast. Mouth open, bites her lip. You see the magic in her face.

"I'm really stoned."

She sits with her back to a tree. Tommy takes her back to his place. Her foot is in the camera, lying back. He brings her a cup of coffee but she doesn't drink it. Hands it back to him. They talk about her crazy dad.

"He scares me."

She gets Tommy to do funny impressions. She laughs.

"Do you have any friends?"

They play fight. She wins. Both end up on the floor. He asks if she wants to watch TV.

"No."

Asks if she wants him to take her home.

"No."

They kiss, slow and passionate.

Next morning they ride in his ice cream truck. She is pale again. Hugs herself. She feels weird so he reassures her. Smiles. They kiss, only just. She jumps out of the truck two streets down from her house. Almost forgets her bag.

"Oh shit."

Her dad drives by minutes later, stops Tommy. Asks if he's seen his daughter. Tommy is flustered, says no. Jerry looks at him suspiciously. Goes back to the house, finds Chloe, and lays into her. She cries and locks herself in her room, calls up Tommy. Cradling the phone. You can see the calf. She wants to see Tommy but he is scared. Hangs up on him.

She decides to leave for the city. Her friend Puck is giving her a ride. Tommy catches her as she is loading up the car. Puck likes Tommy and calls him Bro. He is oblivious. Tommy tries to console Chloe but it doesn't work.

"Can we go?"
Those are the last words you hear from her. *Can we go.*
The film goes on for maybe another fifteen minutes, without her.

spun in circles and half-circles and even did a double 360 at one point. The interviewer was already having a horrendous time.

This made the entire audience laugh and kind of gasp.

The auditorium was full. Not one empty chair.

"So I don't get it," Bret said. "You've just spent twenty minutes introducing me, and then at the end of that introduction you say... for a man who needs no introduction."

Red stormed the flustered face of the interviewer.

"I mean, I'm just a dumb American ... I mean, is this what you Brits call irony, right? Are you playing with irony here or was that just a knucklehead moment?"

I didn't know the guy next to me, but he leaned in mid-laugh and said, "I think he's on cocaine."

I didn't care about that. I just felt the copy of *this* novel on the inside of my jacket. I had been checking it every ten minutes for the last three hours.

"So how have you been Bret?" The interviewer suddenly strengthened his voice and opened himself up, attempting to shake away those early-interview, starstruck nerves. "How is your UK tour going thus far?"

Bret did another 360 and then stopped dead on his feet. "Awful," he said. "Just awful. I hate these fucking things."

Again the audience laughed. I think at this point we couldn't decide if he was being real or if this was a part of his act, a character he was playing. My guess is it was probably a bit of both.

"I'm depressed," he announced.

"Well I'm sorry to hear that Bret. We'll try and get you through this as painlessly as possible."

It was at this point that Bret just waved him off and then gazed into the crowd. It went weird for a while as he silently scanned the room. The interviewer squirming to his left, not knowing what to say.

"What a thing," Bret mumbled searchingly. "A sea of faces ... probably a thousand eyes out there ... looking at you ... all at once."

Eventually his head stopped, and he looked, right at, *me*.

We were here in the strange squinty light.

Guy Next to Me started to fidget. "Shit," he whispered, "he know you or something?"

My reply was to release *this* novel from my jacket only it was stuck.

Somehow the interviewer brought it back but my mind was all-taken-over and I couldn't concentrate on a single word.

An hour went by.

"Okay," Bret kind of shouted, slapping his thigh. "I'm bored now, Can we get to the Q&A. I've got a limousine to catch."

Again the audience found this hilarious and by now the interviewer had *given up* and was enjoying it all.

"So," Bret said. "Questions. "Who's going first?"

My hand shot up so fast and so aggressive it took the audience's breath back. Guy Next to Me went white as the spotlight lit us up.

"Wow. Eager." Bret sang "Okay stalker fan, what is it?"

I had started talking before the microphone had a chance to get to me. It was disturbing to hear my voice sounding like this, so loud and so strained.

"Your masterpiece is considered one of the greatest novels of all-time," I said. "But where *exactly* would you say it ranks?"

Bret was already laughing. "What, you mean like an exact number?"

The audience added to his laughter with their own.

"Oh … ha." This question had really tickled him and this was the first time he had displayed any kind of positive emotion all evening. "Ha, well, let me see now. Where do I rank myself, an exact number. Well I'd have to say 94th. Yes 94th. I've written the 94th Greatest Novel of All-time. Ha, Jesus. Jeez."

A riot of laughter which seemed to go on for minutes. Bret had to take himself to the corner of the stage for a few moments.

I was happy with the answer and stroked *this* book proudly through my jacket.

"Next question," Bret said.

Another hour went by and when I heard, "okay one more." I got up promptly and started to move slowly to the front of the auditorium. Some of the people were looking at me, I could tell. I had timed it perfectly, got to the front, literally as the book-signing started, first in the queue.

Bret was wiping his forehead and sipping a water, fixing his suit jacket slightly.

My own jacket was crippling me because I couldn't get *this* out of my pocket.

He looked up and our eyes met. He looked serious for some reason. "Oh, you," he said, a bit pissed-off.

"I have written a novel." I said. "And I want to sign a copy for you."

Bret paid no attention whatsoever, just took more water. I started reaching to the inside pocket again but *this* was still jammed, trapped in the corner of the lining somehow. I heard a slight tear in the material.

Bret wiped his forehead and waited. Queue was getting impatient and Bret was trying to work out what was going on.

"It really is a great novel," I said.

"Thanks," he said, unnaturally.

"I meant mine ... I was talking about my novel. *This* novel."

By now I was pretty much ripping my whole jacket apart.

Bret started to look around him, his head movements getting a little faster. He had moved his chair back an inch and was about to stand up.

"Here it is," I said at last, out of breath. "This Weirdish Wild Space."

Bret looked exhausted and he blinked hard twice, taking *this* into his left hand, as

I gave it to him with my right. I remember thinking how sensational all that looked.

How We Met

Amber saved my life.

Although she doesn't know it.
That's actually how we met.
Like I said at the very beginning, I almost checked-out at 27.
I was all set.
Decision made.
On my way to the five-story car park without a parachute.
Even had the one-word suicide note tucked into my jacket pocket, *Whoops*...
Heard her before I saw her.
"Fuck!"
Little redhead with a split shopping bag.
Oranges rolling everywhere.
She looked ridiculous trying to pick them all back up.
One headed towards me, magnetically.
Stopped it with my foot.
Picked it up.
Started unpeeling.
"Hey that's ACTUALLY my orange."
"*My* orange now."
She was carrying some of the oranges.
Two bulged from her pockets.
The rest just sort of did their own thing.
She stood before me, dumb.
Like she'd seen a ghost.
She was nervous, for sure.
Her hands were shaking, almost dropped the oranges, *again*.
I was eating the segments by now, mouth full.
Juice on my chin.
"I'm fucking starving."
"Me too," she said.
I was looking at her and she was looking at me and my guess is she was falling in love.
"I'm cooking dinner when I get home you can join me," she said in one sentence.
Then slapped her own forehead with the palm of her hand, dropping an orange.

Let it roll.

"I've just invited a complete stranger to dinner I'm crazy." Again in one sentence.

"I'd love to," I said, clapping my hands.

Then wiping the excess juice on my jeans.

Straight away I had her down for one of these arty types.

Gifted.

Tortured.

Lost.

"No," she said, stopping herself. "I don't know you."

I gave her my name.

Then hand.

She took it, still trembling.

A murmur: "Amber."

"Let's go," I said, heading to her car.

She followed.

"Where's *your* car?" she said.

"I don't have a car."

"What are you doing in a car park then?"

"On my way to the roof," I said, pointing up.

"What for?"

"Jump off."

She burst out laughing, dropped another orange.

By now there were only two left.

"You're ACTUALLY mad."

"You're throwing oranges all over the place and asking strangers back to your house and you call *me* crazy."

"I never said *I* wasn't crazy."

"Crazy together then. Meant to be."

She was sitting at the wheel, fingers pinching the key.

"What am I doing? You could be a psychopath."

"Shut up and drive."

Our Newest Member

You saved his life although you don't know it. You thought he was joking the whole time.

"I'm not depressed," he said, looking out the car window, then back at you. "Don't feel down or sad or angry. Nothing like that. I just see it all as a bit pointless. So like the Flatliners film: *today is a good day to die.* Plus. I'm 27. So I get to join the club."

"What club?" You say, trying to concentrate on *This Weirdish Wild Space* up ahead.

He decides to unclip his seatbelt, and then you automatically do the same.

"Hendrix. Morrison. Joplin. Jones. Cobain. And our newest arrival ... an angel if there ever was one ... Miss ... Amy ... Winehouse!"

"I don't know what you're talking about," You say.

"This is the company I keep," he says.

He makes you smile. He makes you laugh. He relaxes you in a way like never before. He gets in-tune with you, like, *straight away.* Like you've known each other for years. A whole lifetime. His humour calms you, takes you out of yourself. You've been down for days, weeks. Down, down. But he has brought you up, *up.* This slice of madness is exactly what you need. Something random and spontaneous to lift you out of the quagmire.

"Literally," he says. "Your oranges have *literally* saved my life. *You* have saved my life. And you know how it works. You know the rules. I am responsible for you now."

You laugh all the way home.

"I'm vegetarian," You tell him, shutting off the engine. "That alright?"

"Not ideal. But it'll have to do."

His handsomeness no longer intimidates you. You have stopped trembling, *finally.* You have met a friend, a soul-mate it seems, in the most unusual of ways.

A Mother Inside The TV

The TV is crying.

There is a woman inside it.
Her fringe is hard but her face is soft.
Soft with grief.
Split open with grief.
Trauma rips through it and it's difficult to watch.
But I do, watch.
I have to.
Her son has been missing for four days now and it doesn't look –
It looks unlikely that –
I pull up a chair and sit opposite her.
This beaten woman.
This poor –
I pop a bag of popcorn and toss them into my mouth, one at a time.
Then I get up and go to the fridge and pour a large glass of cold milk and return to the TV and watch this poor woman plead and grieve and beg into the screen and then she looks up and seems to mutter something at the sky and I think *who is she talking to?*
Suddenly the curtain moves behind me and I realise I've left the window open.
It's still winter outside, the last day of it.
February 29th.
This day only happens once every four years.
I think about that.
I think about *invisibility*.
Of things existing even though we can't see them.
I drink the milk.
I watch the TV and the mother inside it.
I turn down the sound and I think about my own mother and my own son who hasn't been born yet and imagine what it must be like.
To lose one.
You don't know until you know, they say.
And I guess that much is true.
So I close my eyes and travel over the oceans of time.
All the sons and all the daughters and all the mothers and all the

fathers and all the wars and all the births and deaths that have been and are still to come.

I see a tree fall and a baby pop out.

I see the eye of an eagle and a fire burning a house down.

I see a waterfall, and more sky, space.

I see –

I hear –

I open my eyes and the woman inside the TV is gone and what has replaced it is a film from the 1980's.

They're all in this one: Emilio Estevez, Rob Lowe, Demi Moore, Ally Sheedy, Judd Nelson, Andrew McCarthy, Andie MacDowell.

I turn the volume up and watch it.

The plot and the characters are so ridiculous that the film is so bad it becomes good.

And this makes me truly laugh and enjoy it.

After I turn the TV off and stare into it for a while.

I watch the outline of my dark, featureless reflection.

I drink the milk and the curtain flaps behind me and I know I have seen this scene before, somewhere in another film.

Before I know it midnight comes and now it is the first of March.

First day of spring.

You

I saw you this evening.

About an hour ago. It was getting dark. Too dark to be walking alone.

You were just coming out of Tesco Express with a shopping bag in each hand. The bags looked heavy and it made you walk funny, like a penguin. My first instinct was to speak. Say your name. But then something else told me to be quiet. I watched you walk on, waddle on. You looked cute, oblivious, in your own world. You had to keep stopping to give your arms a rest. When you stopped, I stopped. You'd look at the lines on your hands and then rub them on your jeans. Pick the bags back up and set off again. When we got to the bottom of Apple Tree Lane you stopped to put your earphones in. I couldn't believe it. It was almost dark and now you were putting earphones in. I now knew I had to follow you all the way home. There was no way I could let you walk this jitty alone. Not like this. Not at this time. You walked past a bus stop with a billboard. You were staring right into it and I swear you could see me through its reflection, following you.

At the foot of the jitty you stopped one last time. Put your bags down and took your earphones out and waited. Waited longer than all the other times. It's like you knew someone was there, *here*. A strong wind came from nowhere and blew your hair. Blew the grass and the leaves on the trees. Although I couldn't see your face I knew you had your eyes closed and was taking it all in. Feeling it on your face. The whooshing sound in your ears. It was electric. Everything was alive.

You started walking again so I started walking again.

Only something fell from your bag and slapped on the floor. It was a book. This book. *This Weirdish Wild Space*. I watched the cover flicker in the wind, before bending down to pick it up. I opened it at the bookmark and read on...

You started walking again so I started walking again. Shadows fell off your feet like stilts. You were almost at your front door. A cat jumped up the wall and you stroked and talked to it. It took you ages to find your keys. I watched you unlock your door and step inside. Lights went on and you were home at last. Safe and sound.

I waited around for a few minutes before tip-toeing up to your door and posting this book.

The letterbox makes you jump and you almost drop the mug you're about to put by the kettle. Wearily you step along the hallway to see a familiar book lying face-down on the mat. You bend down and turn it over and see ...

This Weirdish Wild Space

Joe Cassius

Drink The Coffee While It's Hot

My letterbox goes clap and makes me jump. I almost drop my Superman mug on the kitchen floor. Instead I put it next to the steaming kettle and head down the hallway. Amber has sent me a book which makes no sense because I don't read and she *can't* read. On the inside of the jacket, between the pages, is one of her handwritten letters. I notice Amber has started sending me letters on the first of every month. She's OCD, too. I forgot to tell you that. She has a thing for numbers, dates, repetition. Says it's a control thing. Helps with the dyslexia and the bi-polar, she says. I open the envelope. Think her printer is broke again.

FUCKING PRINTOR IZ BROAK AGEN!!!

Funny. The only word she gets right, *fucking*.

So bear with me again. So how are you? Hows it bean. Me and Ben are ACTUALLY still going strong and its almost been six months now and I cant believe I havent seen you in eight thats fucking mental and I think the last time was your mums birth day witch you forgot and you dint even go to the cemitry or where they scattered her ashes but then I needunt be surprised. We ate at that shit restoreant remember and looked at my old office and then I went to by some clothes but just ended up looking at thme for like three hours. You are patient with me ill give you that. Four all your falts you are pateint. The very last time I saw you you were on the bus but I don't think you cud see me. mad. never new that wud be the very last time god life is crazy. Ben knows little about us and our passed and rarely id like to keep it that way. Jesus he bys me so much I know that doesnt really meen anything but sometimes its just good to be spolit every once in a while yknow shit ill never forget how we met and wot happed and it was all down to a ripped shopping bag just think if that bag hadnt split at that EXACT moment then we may never have ACTUALLY met. Shit. Shit shit I was so nervus and I ACTUALLY invited you back for diner wot woz I thinking well I clearly wasnt. Unreel how nervous I was you were/are so hansum I couldt believe it. Never met anyone like you and will never but this split woz four the best and even tho your not wrting back I know you are thinking aboiut me and wishing me well and oh my exhibition is in three weeks and Ive added three more phtos one is of you where you where you think you look like bradley cooper although I don't see the resemelnse but it's a cute photo anyway ben is comeing with me to the exhibition and all though he hasn't got your artist eye he has been ACTUALLY suppoertive in making connextions and buying me a dress and driving me down there and why didn't you ever lern to drive hey it was allways down to me gosh I shouldt always compare you and ben becarse you are so different and these are different times. Hope you don't mind me writng to you like this its just my way I still miss your mum and dad and still cant beleeve they aint here so trippy and in a fashion I cant wait for this year to end. Any way have you met any one??? Im very intrigued by this becarse your so charming and people are drawn to you yet at the same time your soo weird and I cant ACTUALLY imagine you ever in a relationship and definatly not married. I think ben wants to get married one day and have kids he some times mentions it in passing. Anyway I want to here for you so cud you write me a letter just one to let me know your good I still care.

Ps thank you for helping me write my memowr I really hope we can do more of this one day. You know how shit I am with words and you helped me sososo much!!

Amber Rice x

Apple Tree Lane

You walk up it backwards, leafing through this novel.

You find what you're looking for at the top of page 43.
"It's somewhere around here." You mutter, taking your eye off the page, looking around.
Church spire.
Path.
At the top of it you see her standing there at her garden gate.
Old.
Very old.
She is thin and flaky and unhealthily tanned.
Cross-eyed.
"Michael is that you?" she says.
Looking right at you.
"This novel is going to make me rich," You whisper.
Only you're super nervous because you've never done anything like this before.
So nervous you almost take off.
"Son," she says, desperate.
"Yes," You manage.
For some reason you have made your voice deep.
"Oh son you're late."
"Well I'm here now mother."
She touches your hand and your instinct is to pull back.
"Well come in from the cold."
"Okay."
"Dinner is served."
She turns and walks back into the house.
You look either side, see if anyone is watching.
You're not good at this kind of thing.
Inside her house.
Nothing out of place.
Very opposite to yours.
Follow her through to the kitchen.
Wooden spoon.
Stirs a big pot of stew.
Steam.
Smells like hell.

Serves up.
You sit, trays on lap.
You're not hungry but you know you have to go along with this.
A sudden attack of guilt, shame.
Thinking of your own grandma who is dead now.
Fuck it, you think, you *need* this.
"Enjoying that son?"
"Very much," You lie.
You notice a photo.
Her a few years back with a big fat boy.
He doesn't want to be there.
You can tell.
Yet she is oblivious, naïve.
Like *now*.
"Will you get that kitchen knife?" she asks.
"What for?"
"Cut up the cake."
You pick it up.
Feels overwhelming in your hand.
Light handle.
Heavy blade.
Sweating so much it feels like it's about to slip.
Your mind, too, feels like it's about to *slip*.
You eat the cake and sit back.
She points the remote at the TV and fires it up.
Takes your hand and you watch the 1996 film, *Trees Lounge*.
She dozes off.
Close your eyes too but no sleep, *this is it*.
Unpeel her feathery fingers and stand.
Tip-toe across the room.
Look at that photo again, *it'd only go to that fat ungrateful prick anyway.*
Take out the novel and check.
Page 43, *bottom drawer*.
You open it and are stunned with what's before you.
Four stacks of twenty-pound notes.
And *big* stacks.
Doesn't mention this in the book.
Stacks behind stacks.
Whip off your rucksack and start to fill it.

Imagining a sum as you do, 10, 000, 50, 000, a 100?
You have no idea.
She's snoring now.
String of salvia swinging from her bottom lip.
Nerves are gone.
Mind, clear.
Hand, steady.
Purpose, pure.
Remorse, none.
Guilt, gone.
You are free.
You lean over and kiss the old dear on her forehead.
"See ya mama."
Turn and look at the TV, girl at a funeral.
You leave the house.
The garden.

Apple Tree Lane.

Dream

Chloe spoke to me last night. Somewhere around 3am, I think. She was riding a white horse bareback and she said, *keep talking.* Jumped off the horse and came right up to me. Her eyes were extra dark and her skin was extra pale and her hair was extra blonde. Her smile was peaceful as always and she said, *Megan only gets half the picture. You get it all. If only you slow down a little we might make it through the night.* We sat in a red room and she draped her legs over me. I looked at her calf but knew that now was not the time. *Massage my feet,* she said. I did. Her feet made me think of dolphins. *Mermaid,* I whispered. She closed her eyes and purred at my touch. Head back, exposing her throat. When I stopped she opened her eyes and looked at me and said, *I'm pregnant.*

You Don't Like Joe

You don't like Cassius.

    You don't like Joe Cassius.
    You don't like his name.
    You don't like his hair or his clothes or his shoes or his friends.
    You don't like the way he talks.
    You don't like the way he lives.
    You don't like his mind or what he stands for.
    Most of all you don't like *this*, his art, this book, his novel, these words.
    You don't like the title.
    It doesn't make sense to you.
    You want something else.
    You want to call it something else, rename it.
    Something apt. Something new.
    Something that means something to you.
    As the reader you should be allowed.
    You have that right.
    So you close the book up and look at the ceiling, the tree above you.
    Your eyes roam as you think up a new title for this.
    Think about the story and who's in it and what it all means.
    Then it comes in an instant, a flash, a lightbulb moment.
    You're happy with what you've picked.

    Happy with the new front cover.

Chloe's Calf

Joe Cassius

Dedicated to Me

"A piece of dust goes a long way.
It's an old story."

Nicholas Elliot

Siesta

This is a good time for us to give Our Hero a chapter off. He could do with a rest, time out. Like *his* hero Ferris Bueller says, "Life moves pretty fast. If you don't stop and look around once in a while, you could miss it."

So let's take a moment and allow him to breathe, stretch, snooze. A page to let him get his head around it all; Chloe, Amber, Orphan. The latter stages of his grieving process for Swayze. The shock of having *this* title suddenly switched.

A lot has happened in 30+ chapters.

So we need to care for Our Hero the way he cares for us.

His light and love and looks and wisdom have been carrying us for 90 pages so now is the time we show a little gratitude.

So nip downstairs and put that kettle on. Throw in a few biscuits. Fluff the cushions. Pull out the footstool. Switch on the fan and stick on a Swayze …

"C'mon hero. Come take a load off."

Siesta Over

Thanks guys.
   Appreciated.

   But,

   I'm ready.
   Ready to battle on for you, again.

   So,

   Turn that page.

   And,

   Let's go.

   Let's do this shit.

Psychopath

I think that maybe I fell in love with you for just one night.

    One night.
    That's it.
    And then it was over.
    I picked you up in a cab and then drove you to the Indian restaurant.
    You had your hair plaited and you looked like a hippy.
    The restaurant was fancy and I could tell you had never been to a place like this before.
    I kind of blew you away.
    We shared a bottle of wine and I looked at you through the flickering candlelight.
    Was surprised by my own feelings.
Atmosphere is a trick to the senses.
    It was our first date.
    The meal went really quick.
    We talked about clever things.
    Philosophy.
    Psychology.
    You said I had traits of the psychopath.
    I said that I didn't know what you were talking about.
    That's another trait, you said.
    But I have *feelings,* I said.
    No, you said, you just *learn* them.
    It was cold outside and we had missed the bus so I decided to pay for another cab home.
    The taxi driver asked us if we'd had a good night.
    So we fooled him by pretending we were on our two-year anniversary.
    He believed us so I told him more and more.
    You were impressed by how convincing and elaborate I was.
    You have talent, you said.
    At home we dimmed the lights and got under a blanket.
    I held your legs, felt the shape of your calves.
    We talked about the perfect life together.
    A life in rural France.
    Idle coffee shop mornings.

A farm.
Kids and animals.
Green fields and blue skies.
And that's the moment I fell in love with you.
Right there and then.
I got in your bed and put your pyjamas on.
Faked sleep but you came in and woke me up and said, *you can't stay here.*
So I told you we were just friends who could hold each other but you said *no.*
Anyway my own bed was much bigger and better but still I wore your pyjamas.
In the morning you were in the kitchen fixing coffee.
And I looked at you through the flickering sunlight and thought,

Why did I fall in love with you, my own lover is much better.

Letter

Dearest Amber,

You are so special it stings.
   Life is good, with us.
   You and I are cool, we're just doing our thing.
   Glad you're happy and we know how talented a photographer you are.
   Fuck words.
   We have enough words.
   What the world needs now is pictures.

   Your pictures.

   Much love, Me. X

My Literary Agent

Meet you at Sloppy Joe's.

Soho.
The first thing I see are your knees.
You stand when I arrive.
"Hello."
We hug.
Take off your sunglasses and I take off mine.
Haven't seen your eyes for ages.
You look younger.
"Stop tryna flatter me," You say.
Can't win.
"I don't wanna eat here," You say. "I just like the name."
We go two doors down to a lobster joint.
"My treat," You sing, sweeping up a menu from the outside table.
Inside is cool.
"Lobster lunch?" I say. "What old granny have *you* been robbing?"
You look at me half shock/half dread, like you've been caught-out.
Waiter takes us to a table.
Me: back to the wall.
You: back to the action.
"Wanna switch?" I ask.
"What d'ya mean?"
"Some people can't sit with their back facing."
"I'm good."
Waiter brings us our drinks and then sits next to me.
"Make yourself at home," I say.
You laugh.
"Sorry," he says, blushing a touch. "I just wanted to explain the menu to you guys."
He does.
In the end I just point to option two.
You have the same.
"How's your first lobster experience?"
"Horrific," I say.
"Ha."

"Don't know whether to eat it or fight the fucking thing."
"Tough?"
"Never been attacked by food before."
"Now," You say, changing the subject, placing your palms on the table. "Your novel."
I hold up a claw, inspect it.
"This Weirdish Wild Space."
"Chloe's Calf." I correct, sipping the coke. "The title has been changed, remember?"
"Whatever."
There's people moving about behind you. I can't concentrate.
"I've read the first half, maybe."
"You have?"
"I don't like it," You say suddenly, decisively.
"You don't?"
"I don't get it."
"Maybe I should have brought you roses?"
"It *tries* too much. *You* try too much."
The lobster is gone but I'm still fucking starving.
"Tries to be too clever. Tries to be too weird."
"Oh."
"I mean what was all that shit about Patrick Swayze?"
"The world hasn't been the same since."
"It's all over the place."
"Omnipresent?"
"Some could say it was pretentious."
I look at the menu for something lobster-free.
"It has no real plot, structure. It simply isn't *focussed*. I don't like the title. I don't like the main character. I don't *feel* him. I don't *feel* his journey. And Chloe. Who *is* Chloe? Does she *ever* talk? You can't have a lead character that never talks."
"Can we go back to Joe's?"
"There's too much white space, too. It needs more meat."
"*I* need more meat. Burger or something."
"I think you should write something else."
"What do you recommend?"

"Anything. But *this*."

Letter

Dear Chloe,

This is probably the craziest thing ever. But I have an instinct that you live here, in this turquoise house. Even though the chances are probably like a billion to one. But, I'd thought I'd take a shot.
   I love you.
   And I feel this weirdish wild connection.
   Ah, Chloe.
   I know you know and I guess there's not much we can do but let it play out.
   I woke up this morning and there were fingerprints on my window.

   Have you been visiting me, too?

   Anyway, I'll see you around.

   X

Comedy God

Broke into your house last night.

    This invisible lock-trick I do.
    Leaves not a trace.
    Step inside you.
    Your house.
    Your place.
    Your home.
    Your space.
    I opened your fridge and was invaded by light.
    It lit me up like a god.
    I looked like a Greek one.
    Standing in your kitchen with my shirt off.
    Drinking milk from the carton.
    Gulp.
    Gulp.
    A drop landed on my chest.
    Wiped my mouth.
    And headed upstairs.
    Towards you.
    I know you live alone.
    Not even a cat.
    I remember your landing.
    Just how long it is.
    Like a hotel corridor.
    Your door at the end of it.
    Ajar.
    I breathe in.
    Slip in.
    Inside your room.
    The shape of you hovers in the moonlight.
    You look perfect.
    Perfectly placed.
    Pristine.
    Serene.
    You look dead.
    You look beautiful.
    Dead beautiful.

I stand over you and watch.
Watch over you like I have been your whole life.
Skin looks so soft.
Like.
I could put my hand right through and feel deeper.
The deepest part of you.
"Isn't this supposed to be a comedy?" I say.
Hand over my own mouth.
hush
You can't hear me.
You don't stir.
I take a closer look to see R.E.M.
Not the band but that crazy eye-flicker that dreaming dogs do.
You are a dreaming dog.
Dreaming of me.
Of how we used to be.
Our past.
Our youth.
Our tender nights.
I touch your forehead.
You know I'm *here*.
My hand resting over the surface of your thoughts.
The moon is full.
It presses against the curtain and gives us something.
unpeels us
It's powerful tonight.
A powerful night.
Out there and in here.
Always that breeze.
World turning.
Life in slow-mo.
Life on re-peat.
We've been here before.
And we'll be here again.
In your room.
In your head.
I live here.
Worked my way into present tense.
Did you notice?
Have you noticed?

Time to leave you there.
Back out your room.
Back across your corridor.
Back down your stairs.
Back into your fridge.
More milk.
Open the door.
Close your door.
Back into the night.
In the morning you'll wake from a crazy dream.
Something will feel odd.
Amiss.
Something missing.
Something gained.

In the kitchen you'll open the fridge and take the carton and hold it up to the morning light.

I am on your lips.

People

People. Can't describe the vibe I get when I'm around them. *Ah.* I just want to be around people all the time. They say money makes the world go round but they are wrong. People do. People make the world go round. I know. I know because I've seen it. I know because I've lived it. I know people. I *feel* people. I love people. I love to know them. Find out about them. I do this very quickly. It's amazing really. It's amazing how I do this. You should see me. You should watch me *go*. People tell me things. People open up. Sure they open up. I can turn strangers into friends within minutes. *Literally* minutes. I guess you could say it's something I was born with. Some people can cook. Some people can dance. Some people have other things going on. But I have people. I'll meet someone somewhere. In a waiting room or a coffee shop. I'll start off with something light and funny. Before you know it they are telling me *everything*. They are hooked and locked-in. Moving. Moving towards something. Moving towards something with me. Something, *together*. People. I take them as I find them. Let them be. Let them be *exactly* who they are. Mould myself around them. Like a shape-shifter, a chameleon. I'll start to open up. And then they'll start to open up. They'll see me open up and then they'll do the same. People want to be this way but they are scared. That's where I come in. I enable. I facilitate. I provide an experience. I provide a service. Free of charge. They have my time. They have my mind. As I have theirs. Very quickly I tap into the core of who they are and what they want. I do this because I love them. I do this because I love people. I want to gobble them up. Devour them in full. People and more people. There's never enough. As one leaves another arrives. They are brought to me and placed at my feet. Almost by appointment. I am not a person. I am people.

You

Mouthwash for breakfast.

You haven't eaten properly in days.
Not slept much either.
But, you feel fine.
Nothing to worry about.
It's 11am and you decide to leave the house.
Hit town.
Do some shopping.
Haircut.
Tanning salon, perhaps.
Vanity Day, you coin it.
You do all the above and feel better for it.
Look better.
You're supposed to be off-sick so you keep one eye open.
Hope no one sees you.
At last you get your appetite back.
Take a light lunch somewhere, small fish dish and a tall glass of orange juice.
Cinnamon tea while you flip through the novel you've just bought, *Chloe's Calf.*
After you float around the new shopping centre, American-style mall.
A familiar face in the crowd.
Two, in fact.
Megan and her girlfriend Clare.
No.
Not Clare.
Chloe.
Chloe, you note the coincidence to the novel you've purchased.
Megan lights up.
Arms open like she's known you a lifetime.
Takes you in them.
Big breasts.
Big arms.
Big squeeze.
Feels good.

Chloe stands back, looking at the floor, blonde quiff pointing at her shoes.

"We're going for a drink!" Megan announces.

"Great," You say. "There's a coffee shop …"

"I said *drink*."

Megan is a rock star.

She has the atavistic charisma of her cousin.

Wine bar.

Megan orders a bottle of it for both of you.

Chloe takes water, still.

She sits there, lifeless.

What Megan sees in her is a mystery to you.

Pale.

Thin.

Ill-looking.

The words *bland, insipid,* come to mind.

She has that corpse quality, dug-up.

She's not talking again.

You wonder:

Medically mute or plain old rude?

You hear she's some kind of actress so you diagnose her with *contrived coolness.*

Thinks she's some kind of Andy Warhol or something.

After a while she touches Megan on the arm and nods to the door.

"You heading off babe. I'm finishing the bottle, and then some."

Chloe doesn't seem to mind.

You wonder if she has any feelings at all.

Watch her leave and you feel anger towards her but you don't know why.

"And then there was two."

Megan looks at you.

You at her.

You're here, alone together, with this bottle.

Introducing Megan Properly

This girl got morbidly obese, like of the can't-get-out-of-the-couch variety. Then she took a picture of herself and posted it next to one when she was 19 and ridiculously hot. Caption overhead: FUCK-EM. She did this as a two-finger salute to these image-conscious times.

Guess she showed them.

A Day to Myself

Used to be an elitist, but I'm so above that now.

    Been eating a shit-load lately.
    And slept like a baby.
    It's 11am and I leave the house.
    Hit town.
    Do some shopping.
    Haircut.
    Tanning salon.
    Look and feel a million $
    Just another day at the office.
    Maybe I should start thinking about getting a job.
    Or not.
    Hungry again.
    Take a large mixed-grill and a tall glass of orange juice.
    Cappuccino while I leaf through, *Infinite Jest.*
    After I float around the new shopping centre.
    And then I see her, *Chloe.*
    Just knew I would today.
    Woke up and felt her.
    Felt her in my bones and in my spirit.
    The sight of her is obscured by Megan.
    Who pulls me into a big-breasted hug.
    Squeezes the shit out of me.
    Through her hair I watch Chloe.
    Looking at the floor, blonde quiff pointed at her shoes.
    "Let's go for a drink," I say.
    Megan is always laughing. "Took the words right out of my mouth."
    "Meatloaf." I say.
    "Ha."
    Wine bar.
    I order a bottle of still water for Chloe and I.
    Megan takes a wine.
    I no longer feel nervous around her.
    I'm centred.
    Slow.
    Silent.

Feel like a shark.
"I saw your film."
Looks at me.
"You were good."
Says *thank you* by pursing her lips, nodding.
"Be honest," Megan says. "Am I getting fat?"
"Yes," I say. "You are."
"Good."
Chloe is still looking at me.
"That's the plan," Megan continues. "I'm working on something."
"Working on what?" I say.
"Going for a piss and then I'll tell you."
She gets up.
And goes.
First time Chloe and I have been alone.
We don't look at each other but we don't look away from each other either.
There's an Elvis clock on the wall.
I watch a minute go by as his hips sway to the passing of seconds.
"Get my letter?" I say.
Looks at me.
Her eyes smile.
That deep, deep eye contact of hers.

Nods.

The Art of Self-Reflection

"You need to write a novel," You say, laying on the bed next to me.

"What?" I've just woken up, or just dropping off. I don't remember which.

"You need to write a novel."

"Who?"

"You."

I sit up and look at you, your face is so close it's like we're gonna kiss.

"What are you talking about?"

"I've been thinking about it and I think it could be your thing."

"My thing?"

"Everyone has a thing and this could be yours."

I look out the window and see that couple again, handsome guy and ghostly girl.

They walk between these sentences and head for the hills.

"What would I write about?" I say.

"People."

"What?"

"You're always talking about how much you love people, adore people. How you're addicted to people. So why not write about people?"

I look at you but it's like you're not really there, like you're just a half-thing fading in and out.

I get up and put the kettle on. Part of me still feels asleep and I wonder if I'm dreaming.

Then I wonder if it's you that's dreaming.

"It's just a suggestion," You say, looking at your watch.

"Thanks," I reply. "But novels aren't real. Imagination is not something you can put your finger on."

The kettle is boiled and I have made you a cup of tea, only there's no one to hand it to.

River Phoenix

I was there when River Phoenix died. Sad time. Poor fucker didn't have a chance. He was looking right into my eyes as he drew his last breath.

"Hang in brother."

"I can't," he said.

It sounded like he was having a shit.

"Let it go then," I said.

Suddenly he looked scared. He coughed up something. I moved a strand of hair from his eyes.

"Is this a scene in a film?" he said.

"Nah. It's a scene in a book."

"So I'm not really dy …"

Remy LaCroix

I seemed to be the only one in The Midnight Bar who didn't know who she was. She had flown in from America but I still didn't know who she was. She looked about 14-years-old and couldn't stop laughing when she saw me.

"But you look nothing like Jason Momoa," she howled. "You look about 18-years-old. Jason is a fucking man! *The man.* Never has a man been so man and you look about 18-years-old."

I laughed too cos what she was saying was dead right.

"I have to fuck him," she said. "I just *have* to."

"Sorry but I'm having a sustained period of abstinence."

"Is this the only way you get to talk to girls?"

"You'll have to contact my agent."

"I don't have one."

"My literary agent." I said. "Although she doesn't see what all the fuss is."

"I'm with her on that."

"Maybe we can meet this time next year."

She nodded, winced. I could tell that the music was hurting her ears too.

Her hair was so long and her body was so slim and I couldn't see what all the fuss was.

"I don't get what all the fuss is with you," she said. "I don't mean to be mean but – "

"You look like a 14-year-old girl," I said.

"You're very *average* looking," she said, her eyes scanning my face. "In fact you're only average-looking *here.* In America, my hometown especially, without the accent, you'd probably pass for like a 3 or a 4. *If that.* In my hometown even *I'm* only considered average and that depresses the fuck out of me."

"My looks."

"Yeah it's a genetic lottery, totally. I mean people lose their minds over me. I get death threats and love threats, constantly. And I'm *only* average. Imagine if I was Jenna – "

"I know how you feel."

A song came on I liked but the volume ruined everything.

"I have to find a way to meet him, " she said.

"It robs man of perspective," I said.

She nodded. "Yeah, if only they could see the little girl within."

"That's the whole problem right there."

"Madonna summarised perfectly when she said –"

"Oh I tan amazingly this time of year. This conversation would have an entirely different tone."

"Amazing is the word I'd use too, *yes*. I can do amazing things with my hair and my body and my –"

"Mind this music is so fucking loud I can barely hear myself –"

"Fucking, *yes*."

"But you're – "

"But I'm giving it up for a year until – "

"My visa runs out."

She stroked her own arm and circled the ice in her glass seriously. "I once knew a guy who would masturbate to one porn star only. He was monogamous, y'know? He wouldn't even fuck his girlfriend. Anyway he found out she'd O.D,'d on something and died and it totally broke his heart. Now he's impotent."

"Important, definitely."

"Yeah forever. He can't have sex again."

"Oh."

"How sweet is that?"

"Very sweet."

"You just don't get that kind of faithfulness these days."

"You don't."

She stopped talking and I stopped talking and we looked around The Midnight Bar for a bit in silence. Someone must have had a word with the DJ because the music had been turned right down.

"I like it in here," she said.

"Me too."

"I like what you've done with the place."

"Thanks."

"I mean apart from me talking about it. There really hasn't been much sex in here at all, *if any*."

"It's a transcendent novel." I nodded. "I've been telling them from the start."

She poked a finger deep into my ribs. "Hey don't get ahead of yourself smarty-pants. There's still a way to go yet."

" I know," I said dumbly, humbly. "I know."

Back to Basics

You seemed weary about me coming over, but I came anyway.

    Cab.
    Let myself in.
    You hugged me at the door.
    That giant smile of yours that makes your eyes disappear.
    "Drink?"
    "Tea."
    "I've got no milk."
    "You know how I feel about tea."
    "Sorry."
    "Hm."
    "Got biscuits."
    "Biscuits are meaningless without tea."
    "Sorry."
    I wasn't impressed.
    Still not.
    I had bought two big bars of chocolate.
    "Let's get fat."
    "I don't need any help with that," You said, rueful.
    "Actually I thought you'd lost weight."
    "Stop trying to flatter me."
    Can't win.
    You took one sofa and I took the other.
    Never had we felt so far apart.
    Your hair seemed to be blonde and black at the same time, depending on the light.
    You told me about America.
    Showed me photos.
    Tennessee was your favourite state.
    Said you wanted to go back.
    After the pics we went quiet for a while.
    Watched one of those *Twilight* films.
    "How can you watch this shit?" I said. "It's for teenagers."
    "It's just easy-watching."
    "There's nothing easy about it."
    "You're an elitist," You said.
    "I used to be but I'm so above all that now."

You looked at me with chocolate around your mouth.
"We go way back," I said. "You and I."
I joined you on the sofa and began to massage your eyeballs.
"This is nice and weird at the same time," You said. "Strangely nice."
"*Strangely nice*, good title for a novel."
You ate more chocolate.
"Talking of novels. I don't want to say it but I've got to say it."
"What?" I said.
"Yours is fucking brilliant."
"Really?"
"I think you could well qualify as a genius."
"Ya reckon?"
"Fucking certain of it."
I looked in the mirror while I carried on stroking your balls.
Imagined Da Vinci looking back.
Or Beethoven.
Newton.
Galileo.
"How's your eyes?" I asked.
"Feels like heaven."
I stopped.
Flexed my fingers and lay back.
"You can't sleep here tonight," You said.
"You haven't got tea."
"No. I haven't got milk."
We lay in silence for an hour.
An hour of silence.
"What's it like?"
"What?"
"Being in bed with a genius?"

"Dunno. I'll tell you in the morning."

Ben

The phone was ringing with an unfamiliar number but I picked it up anyway, "Yo!"

The voice was male and breathy and kind of choking like the way nervous people are. Said my name.

"Yep. That's me. That is I."

"Listen…"

"I'm listening."

The voice was building up for something.

"I'm Amber's boyfriend."

"My boy Ben what up?"

"First off I'm not your boy and second off how do you know my name?"

"First off I apologise profusely for you being offended by my term of affection and second off Amber told me your name."

"She spoke to you about me?"

"Nope."

"What?"

"Wrote to me about you."

"She fucking what …?"

"Benjamin whatever is the matter?"

"The name's Ben."

"Ben whatever is the matter?"

"I know you wrote to her but she wrote to you, the lying bitch!"

"You seem upset Benji."

"Is she still in love with you?"

"Probably."

"What?"

"Probably yeah. They often are."

"The cheating bitch, I'll kill her."

"Now Bennie you're becoming confused. She's still in love with me but that doesn't mean she's cheated. Not with me, anyway."

"What. Did she cheat on you?"

"Yeah but I don't really play that sport."

"Will you just give me a straight answer?"

"Only if you give me a straight question."

"What?"

"I don't understand the nature of this conversation Benzo. Why did you call? What are you trying to ascertain?"

113

"Why you writing to my girl?"
"Your girl?"
"Yeah she's my girl, not yours."
"Okay. Whatever that means."
"What?"
"You're upset that I wrote a letter to Amber?"
I heard him unfolding paper.
"Dearest Amber … *you are so special it stings … life is good, with us … you and I are cool … we're just doing our own thing … glad you're happy and we know how talented a photographer you are …* blah blah blah blah."

"I don't remember writing four *blahs*."
He coughed.
"You're seeing her behind my back."
"No. I'm not."
"But you said she's still in love with you?"
"Yes. She is."
"How do you know?"
"I feel it."
"The bitch."
"But I feel that she loves you too, in her own way."
"This is fucked."
"Benster. Word of advice. Jealousy is no way for a man to live. It is a wasted emotion. Most emotions are. But jealousy is the worst. You should really think about tossing that fish out of the ship."
"What the fuck are you going on about?"
"Would you say that you're somewhat of an unstable person?"
"Fuck you say to me? You putting me on?"
"Benerino. Tell me what you want?"
"I want you to die."
"Look I don't mind helping you out and all, but that is a request too far."
"You're dead."

The line went dead. He was gone.

Dead Man's Keys

I woke up at the crack of dawn, around 8-8:30.

Went straight to the kettle naturally but found myself fixing coffee instead of tea.
Got the percolator out and everything.
It was just that kind of morning.
Binmen were outside, low in the street.
The sound of grinding machinery and sliding glass.
One of the binmen was singing in a strangely good voice, quite soulful.
Then outside my door and over the corridor there was radio squabble and a slow deep voice.
It was some kind of lively morning.
Knock, knock.
Oh?
I put down the coffee and go answer.
"Sorry to disturb you."
It was a young, tall, hairy policeman who looked kind of sad and scared.
"Good morning," I said.
"Good morning," he said.
The young eyes behind his big hairy face looked unusual.
"Did you notice anything unusual last night?"
"Unusual?"
"Did you go out at all last night?"
"Yes, yes I did actually."
"Do you know what time you came back?"
He seemed new at this.
"Erm..." I worked this out some. "I'd say around 9-9:30."
"And did you notice anything unusual last night, when you came back?"
From nowhere it came back to me.
In a flash: Fuck.
The dead man in the stairwell.
"Oh, yeah. There was a man in the stairwell."
"Yes, there was." The policeman nodded mournfully.
The smell of coffee was now strong in my apartment.
"Did you want to come in?" I said. "Coffee's on."

"No that's alright," he said with an artificial cough.
"He okay?"
"Unfortunately the man passed away."
"I thought he might have."
"Sorry?"
"The man. I thought there was a chance he might be."
"You thought the man might be dead?"
"Yeah he didn't look great to tell you the truth."

The policeman was now blinking his eyes hard and fast.

"He looked about 14% dead," I continued. "But I wasn't sure. I thought I saw his chest move."

"14%?"

The policeman's eyes got small and he might have moved forward an inch.

"I swear his chest moved," I said.

He was moving around on the spot now, peering over my shoulder every once in a while.

"Could you just walk me through what happened?" he said.
"I came back around 10-10:30."
"I thought you said 9?"
"No it was later than that."
"Where had you been?"
"Nowhere."
"What?"
"Everywhere."
"Excuse me?"
"I often go out at night. For a wander. A wonder. Just walk around."
"Okay, and you returned at ..."
"About 11-11:30. Around midnight."
"Midnight?"
"Yeah about midnight."

His radio squabble got louder so he silenced it by covering it with his large hairy hand.

"And then what?"
"And then I let myself into the apartment block and started ascending the stairwell and that's when I saw his keys."
"His keys?"
"Some keys, yeah."
"Okay."

"I picked them up and didn't know what to do with them."

"What do you mean?"

"The keys. I didn't know what to do with them. I mean, if I keep them they won't find them."

"They?"

"Whoever the keys belonged to."

"Okay."

"So I carefully placed them to the side, near the wall. So they can find them."

"And then what?"

"And then I took the next flight of stairs and saw his shoe."

"His shoe?"

"A shoe. So I did the same as the keys. Put them carefully to one side."

"Okay, and then what?"

"Well then I took another flight of stairs and that's when I found him."

The policeman had his fist to his mouth and his eyes were big and he looked concerned.

"I think I thought he was asleep."

"You think?"

"Or drunk."

"Okay."

"Or drunk and asleep."

"What made you think that?"

"I thought I saw his chest move."

"Okay."

"So then I went back downstairs and got his shoe and his keys and put them on his chest."

"Why did you do that?"

"So he can get them when he wakes up, but he didn't."

"No he didn't," he said solemnly.

"Actually I only put his keys on his chest."

"Sorry?"

"The shoe I put by his side."

"What then?"

"Well then I stepped over him and went to bed."

"You stepped over him?"

"I had to. He was in the way."

"Okay."

117

"It was late and I was knackered."
"And you didn't think to call anybody?"
"Like who?"
"Oh I don't know, the police, an ambulance?"
"Well I mean I thought I saw the keys move."
"Sorry?"
"On his chest. I thought I saw his keys move, on his chest."
"Yes."
"I was 14% sure."
He moved his fist from his mouth. "Why 14%?"
"I dunno, it was just the number I had in mind."
"So you were 14% sure he was dead but you didn't think to notify anyone?"
"Or maybe I was 14% sure he was alive and I didn't think there was any point, at that point."
"What?"
"Like it was too late and stuff."
"What?"
"No I definitely thought he was alive, alive and drunk and sleeping. His chest was moving. So was his keys."
He raised his eyes."14%?"
"14%, yeah." I said.
"And what about if it was 18% would you have called then, or 20?"
"I dunno," I said, my voice trailing off, "probably."
He shook his head and seemed to be mad about something.
The policeman said something into his radio.
There was more noise around the building now, a soft commotion.
The policeman gazed down the long corridor. "Did you know this man at all?"
"The dead one?"
"Yes." The policeman seemed tired now.
Must have had a long shift.
"No, I didn't."
"You know anyone on this floor?"
"No."
"Okay."
"You sure you don't want to come in for a cup of Joe?"
"What?"

"A cup of coffee."
"No ... thank you."
"Can I take your details?" he said.
"Of course, " I said. "Any way I can be of assistance."
"Thanks for that," he said, with a pained sarcastic smile.

While I gave him my details an ambulance pulled up and there was a sweet, unfamiliar scent drifting up from the stairwell.

As he descended them I shouted after him.
"His death wasn't in vain, you know?"
"What?" he said, totally bored by now.
"He's being immortalised right *here*."
Policeman exited the scene.

"He died in the name of true art!"

Kids

… I remember … as a kid.

I lived on a close with other kids.
There was this one kid.
Who had to be better than all the other kids.
Have better things.
Bigger things.
Newer.
Faster.
More expensive things.
At Christmas he had the best bike.
At Easter the biggest egg.
At Halloween his parents went all-out.
He liked beating other kids, too.
He had to win.
Had to win at all costs.
No matter what.
In summer one day we had the biggest water-fight ever.
Fought with little plastic water pistols.
You remember them?
Those crappy things you had to fill up by a tiny hole at the back.
The kid fought too only he seemed to be holding something back.
Like he had some trick up his sleeve.
He was smug.
Gloating, like he always was.
Kept running to his mum who was just as smug as he.
Then when all the kids were in the centre of the street I saw his mum mouth the word, *now*.
Kid ran in.
And when he ran back out he was armed with one of those quadruple-barrelled Super Soakers.
Fucking thing looked like a tank.
All the kids screamed and ran away.
The kid was OD'ing on power.
Going fucking nuts.
His face was shaking and he was making these inhuman sounds.

AHHHuuuuuuuwwwwwwooooooooaaaaahhhhhhhh.
Like it was a real war.
And he was winning, well.
Only I didn't get it because we had been playing all day and we were already drenched.
When you're wet you're wet.
We couldn't get any wetter.
Wet was wet.
So when the kid came at me I just simply,
Stopped.
Stood.
Faced him.
"Yeah?" he screamed.
He began to unload the barrels only I quite enjoyed the feeling on my face.
It was a sensation I hadn't yet experienced.
It was, *something different.*
Kid got desperate.
Pumped the shit out of it.
Waved it around.
Hit me point blank.
Eyes large and deranged.
From nowhere I decided to dance.
It felt like the thing to do.
The jet hit me at all angles.
I danced around it.
The sun and the water came together and made a pretty little rainbow around me.
"Muuuuuuuuummm it's not working!!!"
He began to cry.
Mum stood in the kitchen window.
Looked like her world had come apart.
The kids came out of hiding.
Watched on, amazed.
Like I had revealed something to them.
They joined in.
Dancing while he blasted.
Eventually he gave up.
Ran back inside.
We carried on dancing even though it was over.

Even though there was no music.
We danced until we were dry.

Danced until it got dark.

Chloe

I can't believe it! Chloe has replied to my letter! I've put it on the next page for you to read in its entirety…

Letter

Chloe

You

haven't seen me in years.

    I turn up at your front door.
You open it and find me standing there; crying, shivering.
It's raining and I'm hugging myself.
You say my name only I can't talk.
"Come in out of the cold," You say.
Take me into your arms, then inside.
Sit me down.
"Let's get you out of these wet clothes."
"I didn't know where else to turn," I say.
You put a warm cup of tea in my hands.
And.
Look at me with those big old eyes.
After an hour I tell you my story.
"It starts with the death of my poor mother."
Tell you how sudden and obscure and unfair it was.
You hold my hand the whole way through.
Tell you about the funeral.
How awful it was.
How heart-breaking.
How tragic.
"Aunt Aud recited this beautiful poem and Dad chose the perfect song."
I tell you how I sat there after, couldn't move.
Couldn't talk.
People tried to console me but I was lost, a shell, a ghost.
"Four months later my father took his own life."
I watch your eyes widen with shock, hand to your mouth.
"He died of a broken heart."
He's not the only one with a broken heart, I go on to say.
After not seeing my girlfriend for six months I come home to find her in bed with another man.
"That was the straw that broke the camel's back."
I then go on to tell you about her new boyfriend.
This crazy man, how he called me up, threatened my life.
"I'm scared."
You've been listening to me for hours.

You're my rock, as always.

You comfort me and give me invaluable advice.

"You need to get back on that horse. You need to meet someone new. There's plenty more fish in the sea."

"There is?" I say, with hope.

You nod, sagely.

"Time heals."

"It does?"

Nod again.

Amazed at your wisdom.

"Actually I have met someone," I say. "Only it's complicated."

Tell you bits about Chloe.

Already in a relationship.

Doesn't talk.

Giving me mixed signals.

A blank letter.

"What about *your* writing?" You ask.

"Don't," I say. "That's worse than anything."

You're still rubbing my back.

"I'm just under halfway into *this* novel but I hate it. It's garbage. I just can't take it seriously. I'm so close to flushing it all down the toilet. Along with everything else in my life. I look like shit. I feel like shit. Now I'm bothering you with all this..."

"There, there," You say. "Everything is going to be okay."

I believe you.

My Looks

My appearance, I think, has gone next level. Sometimes I wish you could see me. Words can only do so much. To get the real experience of my handsomeness you'd have to come see me, *in flesh*. I can't really describe myself because that would only be vain. Anyways, I'm manly. That much I will say. Very manly. I guess I look like a mixture of Gerard Butler, Russell Crowe and that Jason Statham guy. Something like that. I'm much taller in Real Life. You'd be surprised. On a good day I can reach like 6,2 or 6,3. Any taller than that and I'd just be considered gangly. And *we* don't want that. Now. Don't get me wrong. There is a limit to this handsomeness. Don't go thinking I'm a model or something. My cheekbones aren't high and my features aren't chiselled. But. I am very, very handsome. But this is down to your subjective choice of course. I do know that I am not to everybody's taste. Lots of people *don't* find me attractive. Someone even called me *average* once. (That hurt my feelings.) So, I guess you could say the jury is still out. You. Would. Really. Just have to come and see for yourself.

Escort

She's 6ft in heels.

"You want an hour, yeah?"
Think she's wearing a wig.
"I do."
"Hour's a hundred quid, yeah?"
"That'll work."
Take out five twenties and place them on a glass table.
She scoops them up.
Her eyes are half-closed.
She takes off her clothes.
Her breasts are definitely fake.
But.
Whoever did them did a really good job.
Skin is very pale and there are bruises on her legs.
Her feet are in bad shape yet her hands are spectacular.
Magnificently manicured.
Nails must have cost a bomb.
Maybe more than the tits.
The room is pretty cool, too.
White and fluffy.
Four-poster.
Mini fridge.
Little lights around the window like Christmas.
"Wanna beer?" she says.
"I don't drink," I say.
"Right."
She slaps her thigh.
Sighs.
"What do you want to do with me?"
"Lay on your front."
"Aren't you going to take off *your* clothes?"
"Just lay on your front."
She does.
I take off my coat and roll up my sleeves.
Kick off my boots and place them under the bed.
Touch her foot.
She flinches.

Take her foot and begin to massage it.
I can only see the back of her head but something tells me she is staring at the wall.
Something also tells me she wants to say something but can't think what.
I move up to her calf, work in the thumbs.
Small deep circles.
Feel her whole being begin to relax.
Sink.
I stroke her skin.
Study it.
Every freckle, scar.
She's still confused.
But getting there.
Her body gets warmer, softer.
At the beginning it was cold and tense.
Minds start to drift, hers and mine.
I can smell my own aftershave.
Hands are at the small of her back now.
There's a tattoo there.
One that marks this generation.
Senseless spirals interlinked with more senseless spirals.
I trace my finger over it, twice.
Then up the dip in her spine.
Her eyes open.
A flash of eyelash.
Staring at the wall again.
She's expecting me to do something.
Waiting.
Hint of fear.
No.
Not fear.
Unease.
I go back to the massage.
Eyes close again.
Massage more.
Her back.
Palm glides over the surface.
Up.
Down.

Fingertips knead her shoulder blades.
In and around.
Feel the knots begin to loosen.
Onto and into the nape of her neck.
A small sound floats from her mouth.
I can see the side of her face, it's flame-red.
Blank.
Serene.
Somewhere else.
I've been doing this for an hour.
Or two.
Don't know.
Can't remember.
Hands slow to a stop.
Her whole body hums.
Like an electrical current.
I.
Wrap her up in my arms.
The duvet over us.
It's not a wig, after all.
But real hair.
It shines in the fading sunlight.
Curve of her breast is as white as the pillow.
Makes me think of Chloe's calf.
Her breaths move into a light nasal snore.
I unpeel my arms and legs.
Get out of bed.
And leave her there.

Fast asleep.

Not Sure About This

You're dreaming again. In a bright blue pool. Looks like something out of Hollywood. It's night-time. On the poolside, a discarded bikini. Wet footprints beside it. Get out of the pool and follow them to the beach. Footprints continue in the sand. The sea disappears and the sand turns into snow. Prints go into the dark woods. They lead to a cabin. Open the door and step inside. No one here. A fireplace. A stove. Two tables and two chairs. A giant bookcase along the back wall. There's a book on one of the tables, *Chloe's Calf.* Open it randomly to page 131 and read.

Open it to page 131 and read. This is it. You are here. Reading this sentence. And this one. And this. We could go on. But, we won't.

Close the book. Look around. Open the book again.

You're back. Keep reading and don't close the book again. You're dreaming and you want to wake up only you can't. On the other table there is a gun. You need to use this. It's the only way to stop this dream.

Look over at the other table and indeed there is a gun. You want to use it only you're not convinced this is a dream. You're not even convinced this is a book. The whole world of fiction, reality and dream seems to blur. You look at the book. You look at the gun. You rub your eyes and try to open your eyes but you can't. Pick up the gun. Place it at your head.

My Parents Are Peter Sutcliffe and Yoko Ono

They got married in the summer of 1976. They say it was the hottest summer on record but I can't prove this because I wasn't there. The sun hammered down, they said, from the beginning of April right through to the backend of September. A long burning summer under a magnifying glass. When it rained (at last) people took to the streets and had a massive water fight.

I have a picture of my dad picking my mum up in her wedding dress.

For a while I had this picture nailed to my wall.

People would come over and say things like:

"Your dad looks like a killer in his suit."
"Didn't know your mum was Chinese or Japanese."

Letter

Dear Death Boy,

Wear the fuck are you. This is worrying I wood be worried if I thought you had falling out with me but your not the falling out type so I guess this is a different kind of worrying. Printer fixed again so you don't have to injure my atrocious spelling.
 WHERE ARE YOU!!"
Why won't you write back, man.
This is shit.
 I want to tell you about my exhibition n stuff in fact I'm just going to come round your flat cos your either not getting my letters or not reading them either way this is rude you have been like my sole mate for like years and I need to talk and you promised that you'd all ways be there, here.
 AND YOUR NOT!!
 Good job my bipolar isn't playing up or you rarely would be responsible. Anyway. Ben is ACTUALLY acting strange lately. He's been asking all these questions about you. And guys. But mostly about you. It's weird but this behaviour is really starring to bug me and turn me off him like there's nothing more less attractive than a bitchy boy. Huh. Yuk. He asks all sorts of things and tries to be cool but I know he's not witch makes him even less cool, more uncool. Ben is nothing like you. No one is but we know that. You know I'm not the quitting type so I'm not giving up on him yet its not even been a year. But. Accept A knock on your door soon cus this letter business is not working.
 So unless you did send a letter and I didn't get it I don't know. Ether way I love you and see you soon.

PS My spell check has underlined a lot of blue stuff only I don't get it so I ain't even going to try. At least we have spelling so all's good in the hood with that.

 Yours, Life Girl

 xxxxxxxxxxxxxxxxxxxxxxxxxxxxxxxxxxxxxxxx

Me

Your phone rings.
 You pick up.
 "Hello."
 "Who's this?"
 "It's me."
 "Who's me?"
 "It's I."
 You laugh a little, mind rummaging through potential suspects.
 "Okay clown, unmask yourself."
 "Close that book up and come see me."
 You freeze, pull a face, gulp; feel like you're in the film *Scream* or something.
 "How do you know I'm reading?"
 Look out the window, around the room.
 "Because you're reading *me*."
 "What?"
 "I am book."
 "You're crazy."
 "Not crazier than you. You're talking to a book."
 "Is this Chloe?"
 "You got me."
 "Wow. Hi. You alright? Your voice, at last."
 "I'm Megan too."
 "This isn't Megan."
 "And Amber and your Mum."
 "My Mum's dead."
 "So?"
 "I'm hanging up."
 "Maybe I'm Tom Sawyer too. And Jane Eyre and Holden Caulfield."
 "This is insane."
 "Maybe I'm *all* books."
 "What?"
 "I'm omnipresent, man. Omnipresence is cool."
 "What?"
 "Stop reading and come see me."
 "When?"
 "Now."

"Where?"
"Here."
"Uh?"
"Stop reading."
"I can't."
"Why?"
"Cos you keep talking."
"You don't have to listen."
"The words go on."
"You don't have to read them."
"I do."
"Guess you could say I got you under my spell."
"Mm."
"If you won't stop then maybe I will."
"Go on then."
"Okay."

Ben

I like Ben. I do. I like his voice. There's something there. In his voice. There's something in his voice that makes me want to help him. Ben. I believe I can teach him the ways of love. If only he sees past the anger and listens to me. If he listens to me then he might just start to feel better. If he listens to me then he might end up saving Amber. Because I know Amber. And right now she's about two beats away from walking out on him. I know. It's like my hero Ferris Bueller says, "You can't respect someone who kisses your ass. It just doesn't work that way." And Ferris is right.

    Life.

        Just.

            Doesn't.

                Work.

                    That.

                        Way.

You

There's a knock at the door.

    I open it.
You are standing there, smiling and frowning at the same time.
I guess you could say it's *that look.*
"What have you been up to?" I say, like a teacher.
"Nuth-iiiiiiiiiiinn," You say, like a pupil.
The wind is blowing your hair around.
"Gonna let me in?"
I leave the door open and head towards the kettle.
Take out my new matching tea-set and start the tea-making ceremony.
You close the door.
"I've got something to tell you."
"Exciting," I say.
Just as I say *exciting* the wind picks up even more.
A crisp packet flies past the window.
The branches of the tree outside go fucking nuts.
"Kind of exciting, yeah," You say. "But I don't want you to get upset with me."
I look at you.
You bite your lip, and look at the floor.
The tea is ready.
I carry it on a tray into the lounge.
We sit.
You on the sofa, me in my recliner.
I recline.
"You're wearing odd socks," You say.
"I'm an odd person," I reply.
"You *are* that."
"There's a pair just like it, somewhere else."
"Ha."
"Fuck."
"What?"
"Biscuits."
"Oh I'm alright without biscuits."
"I'm not."
I get up and go to the kitchen and open the cupboard and grab

the tin and take it back into the lounge and set it down and pop the lid and grab a Malted Milk and dunk the bastard.

Delicious.

"So," crumbs fall onto my Oakland Raiders jersey. "Hit me with it."

You pause.

Look out the window.

"That wind ain't right. It's freaky. Like a tornado or something."

You take a Malted Milk and dunk.

"Well," You begin. "I was out shopping the other day when I saw Megan and her cousin."

"Chloe?"

I say her name like a flinch response, loud, fast.

"Yeah, Chloe," You say, looking at me strange.

I take hold of myself.

Come back down to earth.

"Well," You pause. "Something happened."

All of a sudden I'm excited, like really fucking excited.

"We went for a glass of wine, which turned into a bottle, which led to a second, which evolved into a third. We ended up in bed."

"Bed with Chloe?"

You pull a face, "yeww, nooo."

"Megan?"

You blush, bite your lip again, look at the floor, nod.

"You slept with my cousin?"

"Yes."

Your mouth is dry.

"Oh."

"Are you mad?"

"Why would I be mad?"

We put our hands in the biscuit tin at the same time.

"I keep listening to 80's ballads."

"So you're in love with her?"

"No. I don't know. Possibly. Probably. *Yes.*"

"That's too many answers."

"I feel bad."

"Why?"

"Chloe, why else?"

The wind has stopped outside.

I wash down half a malt with a swill of tea.

Cough.
Sit back.
"She probably already knows."
"How would she know?"
"People just know things."
"Oh."
We sit silent for a while.
"Have you ever been in love?" You ask.
I feel sick from the biscuits but I dunk another malt anyway and think about Chloe.
Think about Amber.
Think about you.
After a while I snap out of my trance and look up.
You are staring at me.

"Sorry. I forgot to answer."

You and Megan

I really don't mind you being in love with my cousin. Truth is. I think you'll be good for her. But this is *sooo* you, attracted to what is already taken. It's like you get off on the steal. Seduced by *the take away*. It's all about the challenge for you, the risk. You thrive on the drama. To you, life, especially relationships, is like one big movie. Maybe you are nothing without it? I mean you've had partners before. And it's always the same, full-hit, full romance. Then give it a year and your eyes start to wander. See it's not the person you fall in love with, rather the experience, the ambience, the dream you create. You're addicted to the buzz, a new body and mind to play with. Gosh. When will it ever end? Truth is. You've met your match with Megan cos she's exactly the same. Watch *this* space. You could be bad for each other or you could be good. Depends on who gains power first because that's what *all* relationships are based on, *power;* whether we like to admit it or not. Loving is like fighting, whoever gets the first blow in and assumes higher ground usually wins. And by relationships I don't just mean of the romantic kind, *all* relationships have power struggles. It's what makes life so fucking exciting. I mean, even you and I, writer and reader, are battling for power right now as I speak, and you read. Currently I'm winning, but only just.

Amber

There's a knock at the door.

I open it.
Amber is standing there, frowning and smiling at the same time.
She looks excited, nervous.
Her hair is redder.
She's put weight on.
"Gonna let me in?"
I leave the door open and head towards the kettle.
Take out my new matching tea-set and start the tea-making ceremony.
Amber closes the door.
"You don't seem very excited to see me."
Just as she says *excited* the wind picks up even more.
A crisp packet flies past the window.
The branches of the tree outside go crazy.
"I'm excited," I say. "Haven't seen you in months."
She looks at me.
Bites her lip, eyes raise to the ceiling.
"It's been a whole fucking year."
I look at the clock.
"Never been good with time," I say.
The tea is ready.
I carry it on a tray into the lounge.
We sit.
Her on the sofa, me in my recliner.
I recline.
"You're wearing odd socks."
"I'm an odd person," I reply.
"You are *that*."
"There's a pair just like it, somewhere else."
"Ha."
"Fuck."
"What?"
"Biscuits."
"You and your biscuits."
I get up and go to the kitchen and open the cupboard and grab

the tin and take it back into the lounge and set it down and pop the lid and grab a bourbon and dunk the fucker.

Delicious.

"So," crumbs fall onto my New England Patriots jersey. "Hit me with it."

"First off," Amber snaps. "Why didn't you reply to my letters?"

"I did, once."

"I never got it."

"Ben did," I say, biting into another biscuit.

She pulls a face. "What?"

"He must have got to it before you did."

She stands up. "And you know this how?"

"He told me."

She takes a bourbon, bites into it, throws the other half back into the tin.

"What do you mean he told you?"

"On the phone. Said he was going to kill me. Sounded serious too. I believed him."

That old hysteria returns.

She starts pacing the flat, swearing.

Takes out her phone.

"That's it. He's gone far enough. I'm ending it with the bastard."

The wind has stopped outside.

I wash down half a bourbon with a swill of tea.

Cough.

Sit back.

Amber has been ranting down the phone for a good fifteen minutes, without a breather.

She could be talking to an answering machine or she could not be letting him get a word in.

You just can't tell.

"I'm blocking you so there's no point ringing or texting. We're done!"

She hangs up.

Faces me.

Breathes.

Takes a biscuit.

Dunks.

"You should at least give him a say," I say.

"A what?"

"A say, a side, a version of events. He should at least get *a say.*"
"Don't you dare go sticking up for the prick."
"I'm just saying the brother deserves a say."
"*Brother*. He's not your brother. You do know he wants to kill you?"
"Maybe so, but I say, give him a say."
"There's no say. He broke my trust. I can never go back."
"You broke *my* trust, remember?"
"When?" Amber says defiantly.
"Danish Dude."
"That was different."
"How?"
"Well…you don't care."
"I was heartbroken."
She holds up the middle finger.
Let's it hang.
Retracts it at last.
"Have you *ever* been heartbroken?" she asks.
"Of course."
"When?"
"Swayze."
"What?"
"I don't wanna talk about it."
I feel sick from the biscuits but I dunk another bourbon anyway.
We sit silent for a while.
"Can I stay here tonight?" she says, suddenly.
"Sure."
Later I pull her old pillow out from the bottom drawer.

And throw it at her.

Joe Cassius

I got him wrong. Joe Cassius. I got him all wrong. Bumped into him in a second-hand bookshop. He was reading one of his own books.

"You reading Joe Cassius?" I said through a shelf of books.

He blushed.

"I *am* Joe Cassius."

"What?" Could feel my own face stretch with surprise.

"I know. Reading one of my own books. Kind of sad."

"You gonna buy it?"

"That'd be *even* sadder."

"Ha."

I didn't expect him to be a black man but he was. His fro was shaped like an old-fashioned motorcycle helmet. Straight away I liked his smile. It was wide and lovable. From it came a deep, soulful chuckle. Overall he looked like an overweight Denzel Washington. Kind of like Forest Whitaker. Sort of Cuba Gooding Jr. He was a mellow, shy guy. His face looked young but his hair was speckled with dots of grey. I wouldn't be surprised if he was 29 but I wouldn't be surprised if he was 49 either. We walked around the bookshop and carried on talking. Bout books. Bout life. Never had I met a man with such little ego. I mean he was a writer so he had to have some ego, *somewhere*. But, it was hard to detect. He wore second-hand clothes and I can't imagine there were many women around. What did strike me as odd was that he wore a badge with Michelangelo on it. Not the High Renaissance painter. But the Teenage Mutant Ninja Turtle. The orange one who liked to dance and eat pizza. I wanted to ask him about it but we got talking about something else.

"Much money in this writing game?" I asked.

"Not really," he said.

I liked Joe Cassius. I liked his style and I liked his way. I was tempted in asking him to go for a drink. Only I could tell it wasn't his thing and I didn't want to put him on the spot. He seemed like a very private man.

Megan

There's a knock at the door.

    I open it.
Megan is standing there, smiling and frowning at the same time.
She looks nervous, excited.
Her face is red.
She's put on weight, *loads*.
"Let me the fuck in, there's a hurricane out here."
I leave the door open and head towards the kettle.
Take out my new matching tea-set and start the tea-making ceremony.
Megan closes the door.
"I'm excited," she announces.
Just as she says *excited* the wind picks up even more.
A crisp packet flies past the window.
The branches of the tree outside go mad.
"Got something to tell you," she says. "But I have a feeling you already know what it is."
I look at her.
She bites her lip, eyes unmoving.
"What do you think of my weight?" she says suddenly, striking a pose.
"Impressive. Aren't you worried about your health?"
"It's my private experiment, remember?"
I don't remember.
"Forget it," she says.
Can't forget what I can't remember.
The tea is ready.
I carry it on a tray into the lounge.
We sit.
Her on the sofa, me on the recliner.
I recline.
"You're wearing odd socks."
"I'm an odd person," I reply.
"*You* are that."
"There's a pair just like it, somewhere else."
"Ha."
"Fuck."

"What?"

"Biscuits."

"Yes! Go get those fucking biscuits. I need fattening up, *even more*."

I get up and go into the kitchen and open the cupboard and grab the tin and take it back into the lounge and set it down and pop the lid and grab a Jammie Dodger and dunk the c$nt.

Delicious.

"So," crumbs fall onto my New Jersey Jets jersey. "Hit me with it."

"What do you think of me being in love?!"

"Does Chloe know?"

"Chloe knows everything."

I shuffle up the recliner.

"What do you mean?"

Megan eats two biscuits at once, talking with her mouth full.

"Don't be fooled by that dumb, mute routine. She takes it *all* in. Trust me. She knows more than you and I."

The wind has stopped outside.

I wash down half a Dodge with a swill of tea.

Cough.

Sit back.

"But how do you know what she knows, if she never talks?"

Megan looks out of the window, cosmically.

"It's weird. Spend enough time with her and you start to pick up this sixth sense way of communicating."

I don't say anything.

"Maybe you two should be friends," Megan says.

I nod.

"She likes you."

I feel sick from the biscuits but I dunk another Jammie anyway.

"She thinks you're funny."

"I am funny."

"She thinks you're full of shit too."

"I am full of shit too."

"She thinks you're a loving person."

"Does she think I'm handsome?"

Megan has cleared the biscuit tin.

"She doesn't really go in for all that."

"Has she noticed how much I look like Ryan Reynolds?"

She stops crunching, eyes wide.

"You look nothing like Ryan Reynolds."
"Yeah … maybe not today."
Shakes her head.
We sit silent for a while.
Chloe's calf was getting closer.

I could feel it.

Ben

Ben had been in touch, twice. The first time he just screamed down the phone for 20 minutes. The second time was a bit better. We managed to have a civilised conversation.

"You're fucking dead! I swear on my grandma's grave you're dead. I'm going to kill you."

I was eating an apple at the time, green one.

"What's eating you Ben?"

"You stole her from me."

"You need to let go of this possession thing, man."

"You don't know how serious this is?"

I could smell whiskey through the phone.

"Have you been drinking?"

There was a long pause on the other end, confirming the affirmative.

"I'm going to kill you."

"I'd like to help out Ben."

"You can't save yourself"

His voice was creepy. Like in a horror film.

"I'm not bothered about saving myself. I'd just like to save *you*."

"How do you know what I want?"

"Well I'm sure you don't *want* to be feeling like this, all heartbroken and woebegone."

I imagined what he looked like. I pictured brown hair brushed forward. A turtle neck and an earring. Like some character from the year 1996.

"You. Are. Going. To. Die."

"I know."

"You don't take me seriously."

His voice was getting slower. Definitely drunk.

"Oh I do."

"I don't even know what she sees in you. You couldn't give a shit about her. You have no future. No career. You haven't got a job. You need to get a job, loser. You don't even drive. And you don't *have* drive. You haven't got two pennies to rub together."

This much was true. I was broke, again. Waxed will on clothes and good food. A trip to Switzerland. Stayed in a luxury apartment for a week. Top notch. Pool. Giant bed. Balcony overlooking the Alps. Shit. Can't believe I haven't told you about this. May tell you about it properly, in one of the later chaps. We'll see how we go.

"I'm gonna stab you. You took her from me and now I'm gonna take your life from you. I really don't know what she sees in you. Tell me what she sees in you?"

"Looks."

"What?"

"My looks."

"Your looks?" His voice went high when he said that.

"Honestly Ben. My appearance is *ridiculous*."

"Your appearance?"

"Yep. My physical appearance is starting to become offensive. And by this time next year it'll be overwhelming. I wish you could see me. I mean I could tell you about it in words but I dunno man, it just ain't the same. To get the real experience of my handsomeness you'd have to come see me, in flesh. I'm manly. Very manly. That much, I will say. Now Ben I don't want you to get the wrong end of the stick. I'm not a model or anything like that. My cheekbones aren't high and my features aren't chiselled. But. I am very, very handsome. But this is down to your subjective choice, of course. I do know that I am not to everybody's taste. Lots of people don't get it. Lots of people don't get what all the fuss is about. I guess you'd just have to come and see for yourself. Check it out."

"Oh…I'll be coming to see you alright."

"Good. Maybe then we can straighten this thing out face-to-face. I don't mean in a dual kind of a way. More, in a brotherly kind of way. I really do think I can help you. I do."

"Help me?"

"Yes. I will. I will help you with the ways of love."

I couldn't tell if he had put the phone down or not. Either way, there was no sound.

Chloe

There's a knock at the door.

    I open it.
Chloe is standing here.
I kind of expected her, but not.
Her presence has, **impact.**
I freeze.
But I'm on fire.
Lotsa paradox goin down.
Whoa.
Wow.
"How are ya?"
Her face is pale, serene.
She's lost weight.
I leave the door open and head towards the kettle but don't touch it.
    Sit on the worktop instead.
Kind of crouch.
Hands clasped.
The wind closes the door.
Chloe is in my kitchen.
Standing in front of me.
"Want tea?" I say.
Shakes her head.
"Anything to drink?"
She points to the water purifier.
"Good idea," I say.
I pour into two pint glasses.
A crisp packet flies past the window.
The branches of the tree outside go wild.
Chloe calms me.
It's like whenever I first see her I get all fucked-up but within a few minutes I'm the total opposite.
    An ocean.
I lead her into the lounge.
We sit.
Her on the sofa, me on the recliner.
I recline.

"I'm wearing odd socks," I say.
She smiles.
"Maybe because I'm an odd person," I say.
She smiles again, smiles more.
"There's a pair just like it, somewhere else."
She almost laughs.
I recognise her face from the movie she was in.
"Fuck," I say, suddenly.
Her eyes widen.
"Biscuits."
She pulls a face, shakes her head.
"You don't want any?"
Shakes her head faster.
I get up and go into the kitchen and open the cupboard and grab the tin and take it back into the lounge and pop the lid and grab a Hobnob and dunk the little fellow.
Forget that it's water.
Disgusting.
"So," crumbs fall onto my Seattle Seahawks jersey. "Megan told me."
Chloe yawns, closes her eyes.
I wipe my mouth.
"You tired?"
She opens her eyes.
Looks at me.
"Do you get much sleep?"
Holds up an inch between her thumb and forefinger.
"Only a little," I say. "I get lots."
She nods.
"I dream about you," I say.
Gazes at me.
Notice the speckles in her eyes, maybe for the first time.
I don't remember.
Her face says, *me too*.
She puts her leg up.
The shape of her calf hangs over the armrest.
Calfrest.
After a few moments she reaches into the biscuit tin.
Our hands touch.
Electricity shoots through our arms.

The wind has stopped outside.
I wash down half a Hobnob with a swill of water.
"You think I'm funny dontcha?"
She nods.
"You think I'm full of shit too?"
Nods.
"But you think I'm a loving person?"
She takes another Hobnob.
Her eyes never leave mine.
"Haven't you noticed how much I look like Ashton Kutcher?"
Her face spaces out.
Like I'm speaking Ukrainian or something.
Suddenly she gets an itch.
Pulls up her jeans and scratches her calf.

She has no fingernails.

Job Interview

Ben was right. I needed to get a job. Rang around and managed to seal an interview on Friday. I went there.

"Don't look so nervous," they said.

It was a man and a woman.

"So, tell us about yourself?"

"Oh. Wow. Pressure. Ha."

"Maybe just start with your hobbies," the man said.

The woman had sympathy in her smile.

"Okay," I said. "Well. I'm heavily into charity work. My mother passed-away last year so I'm trying to raise money for the support group that helped her. Sponsored walks, treks, that sort of thing. I've also set up a range of fun days and festivals. I just like to put back in, y'know? Make a difference. But I do get to have my own time. It's not all work. I enjoy sports, mainly racket sports, badminton, tennis in the summer. I enjoy socialising too. I go out with friends, to the cinema, meals and things. I'm also a big fan of books. Non-fiction, mostly. I love to learn. I believe there is no limit to learning. Learning is the key to success. Travel. I love travel. Hopefully if I get this job I can pack up that suitcase and see more of this big wide world. To swim with the dolphins in the Great Barrier Reef. That is definitely at the top of my bucket list."

"That's very good," said the woman. "Now your application says you have no previous experience. Tell us, what attributes could you bring to this company?"

"Wow. Well. Obviously since my parents passed I have been out of employment. But a wise friend of mine told me to *get back on that horse*. So that's what I'm doing. Getting back on that horse. And I believe this job could well be, indeed, the horse I am getting back onto. We spend a good portion of our lives at work so why not make that job your second home. And your colleagues … a second family. Sorry … I'm not really answering your question … guess what I'm trying to say is … that I'm motivated, *driven*. I can work independently and also as a part of a team. I'm a quick learner. You give me something to learn and I'll learn it, quickly. I'm a natural leader yet at the same time I respect my superiors, which are you guys."

I waved my hand across them.

The woman wrote something down.

"And where do you see yourself in five years' time?" the man said.

"Alive, hopefully."

We all laughed.

"On a serious note," I said. "Wherever my potential takes me. I'm a big believer in destiny. *What will be, will be*. But at the same time I believe that we make our own destiny. I also believe in living for the moment but with my eyes firmly fixed on the road ahead. It's not the destination, but the journey that counts."

"Wow," said the woman. "Bit of a philosopher."

"Now," said the man. "Who would you say is your idol? Someone you respect and look up to. An inspiration?"

I looked up, thinking, mouthing the word, *inspiration*.

"Got it," I said.

The man and the woman waited.

"Swayze."

"Pardon?" said the man.

"Swayze," I said.

"Sorry," the woman leaned forward.

"Patrick Swayze."

They seemed confused, maybe a touch amused.

"No hear me out," I said. "He really is great. I mean we talk about learning. But this is a man who owned a multitude of talents. He could sing, dance *and* act. I mean, that is some heavy shit…sorry. I meant to say *feat*… heavy feat. Ha. I mean I really could get carried away so I'll reign this one in. All I'll say is he was a very, very loving actor. A true inspiration and we *all* miss him dearly. I mean for me, life hasn't been the same since."

"Okay," they both said, smiling.

"And finally," the woman said. "If you could pick any faults you might have. What would you …"

"I wouldn't!"

The man and the woman were knocked back a bit in their seats.

"Sorry I interrupted you."

"No," the woman held out her hand. "It's fine. Go ahead."

"Well I was going to say, I wouldn't say *faults*. More … *areas of growth*. Every mistake is a lesson. Every weakness is a platform for change. But, if I had to pick one. I mean if I *really* had to pick one. I'd say I'm a perfectionist. For me if it's not a 100% then it's 0%. And that can often get me into trouble. Guess I shouldn't be so hard on myself. Mum used to say I'm my own worst critic. Guess I should curb my eagerness sometimes. But hey. Guess that's just me."

"Okay," said the man.

"Okay," said the woman.

They looked at each other, working out who was going to speak first.

"You're actually the last candidate we're seeing today," said the woman.

"So," said the man. "We'd like to offer you the job."

"Really?" I said.

I felt like there was a tear in my eye.

I made it.

I was, *somebody.*

Instead of this, *nobody.*

First Day on The Job

I lasted a week.

Not even that.
I lasted till Thursday.
Four working days.
Only I didn't work.
Not really.
Guess my demise started on Tuesday when I rolled in at noon.
"Sorry," I said, a little breathless. "Traffic."
"Thought you didn't drive?"
"Thought you lived ten minutes away?"
Couldn't hear them properly.
Had my earphones in listening to Justin Bieber's new album.
Little prick has finally got his shit together.
I'm impressed.
Blown away, in fact.
Love it when people turn it *all* around and silence the critics.
Bieber.
My desk needed some finishing touches.
So I made them.
Inflatable neck-rest attached to chair.
Swishing foot-spa under my table.
Either side of my laptop were two framed photographs.
Left: Swayze.
Right: Chloe's calf.
My colleagues were looking at me strangely, although I couldn't think why.
At 1pm my pizza delivery boy came in.
"One large Hawaiian?"
"That is miiiiiiiiinnnne," I sang in Texan twang.
Revisit Matt McConaughey.
Feet out of spa.
Wet footprints slapping across the office floor.
Twenty quid.
"Keep the change!"
I offered my colleagues a slice but they declined.
It was just past lunch.
They must have eaten already.

Although come to think of it they weren't interested in my bumper bag of biscuits either.

Maybe fitting in is harder than I thought, I thought.

On the Thursday they had me in the office.

Same office.

Same chair.

Same man and woman looking at me.

Only their faces were different this time.

"Your behaviour is a cause of concern."

"What do you mean?" I said. (*Bieber.*)

"You're too familiar with the women," the woman said.

"And the men," the man said.

"Oh. Wow. Well. Like I said in the interview I like to think of my job as a second home ... colleagues a second family."

"It's not how we do things around here," the man said.

"Not how we do things around here," the woman said.

"What does this mean?"

"Means we're going to have to let you go."

"Really?" I said with an intake of breath.

They were both looking at me.

"Let me just take all this in," I said, looking around the room.

We sat silent for a while.

Felt like I needed to say something.

So I did.

"I'm sorry it didn't work out. Maybe if I go away and re-evaluate my performance I can reapply next year."

"That won't be necessary," one of them said.

"Okay."

I felt like there was a tear in my eye.

I left that place.

Crossed the road and stood on the grass and looked at the building for a long time.

It looked kind of forlorn in the flickering, fading sunlight.

This is a Door

You open it and find me in this white room, painting the walls with these words as I go. This word and this word. This sentence. And the next. If I'm not careful I could end up with a whole paragraph.

You move closer, almost tripping on the word **STEP**.

Careful, I say.

You see my face for the first time and you seem a little surprised, if not disappointed.

There is no one else in this room apart from you and I. Writer and reader. Stranger, friend.

This is what a chair looks like. That too is white and you can only just make out the shape of the thing.

Sit, I say, motioning to the chair with my hand.

You do, gently, your eyes never leaving mine.

This is a clock. Only the numbers spiral like a whirlpool and time makes no sense.

This is not what I expected, you say.

Oh?

You're not what I expected. You're not who you say you are. You don't even look the way you say you do.

I sit on the floor cross-legged and listen. You study my face for ages.

You don't look like a movie star, *any* of the movie stars you mention. You're just normal. And you need to stop misleading your readers. You need to stop misleading the people. You need to stop misleading Ben because he's got it into his head that you're some kind of Adonis. Your big fat lie is driving everyone insane.

Oh.

Look, I know you've had a tough time, but you can't be fraudulent like this. You can't pretend you're something you're not.

It's just a story, I say.

I know but even stories have rules.

Do they?

Yes.

What about that chair you're sitting on?

What about it?

What colour is it? I ask.

You look down, to the left and to the right. White, you say.

What about if I changed it to red?

You can't do that, you say.

Look again.

Oh this is what I'm talking about! You say, red-faced, almost as red as the chair you're sitting on. You can't just change things whenever you feel like it. There needs to be rules in life.

Okay.

Look man, I hope it all works out. I hope you get to touch Chloe's calf and I hope it all works out with Ben. Just be a little more honest with who you are and what you look like.

Okay.

Can I go now?

Sure, I say. You're free to do as you please.

You stand and are happy that the chair is white again. You walk across solid ground to the edge of the room. Look at me one last time. This is a door. You open it and leave the room.

Leave this page.

That page.

I yawn and go back to painting the walls with these words. This word and this word.

Another chapter decorated.

Girl

Feel like Jack Nicholson.

    Jack in his younger years.
Five Easy Pieces.
Wayward, wacky and obnoxious.
Hair everywhere.
I stand at the bus stop and wave at cars.
Some wave back.
Some glare.
Most are confused.
I laugh and get on the bus.
Sit at the back, next to the fire exit.
Two stops later a girl gets on.
Hear her before I see her.
"She's a lickle fuckin skank man," she fires into her phone.
I lean out to take a closer look.
Small.
Tracksuit.
Big white trainers.
Chewing gum.
Gold around her neck.
On her fingers.
Hair slapped back into a bun.
"*Nah,* if I see her she's gettin slapped up."
I'm glued to the side profile of her pouting face.
She sits.
Twitchy.
Can't sit still.
"She's a lickle cheeky bitch yeah ... if you see her tump her. Don't say nuffink just dash her in her skull."
Everyone looks at her.
She throws off a round of scowls.
They look away.
I laugh out-loud.
She finishes that conversation and starts another.
Foot tapping.
Phone pressed.
She says the same as before, word for word, more or less.

"Ya better smack her for me yeah. I want nuff gyal on her case."
She phones a third and a forth.
Her foot taps crazy while she waits for them to pick up.
"C'mon you bitch answer."
Someone answers.
Now she's angrier and gives more details.
Like all the other conversations before have wound her up.
Even more.
"Listen to dis Candice yeah y'know dat sket who used to go out wiv Michelle's brother. Ya know her. Lickle tramp wearin her mum's clothes. Yeah. *Her*. She proper just tried to dead-eye me at the bus stop ya know. *Proper*. Telling you yeah I see her again she is gettin beat up. So you tell Kelly and Donique to smack her if they see her and call me when you do."

Conversation ends and she calls someone else.
Foot tapping.
Nothing.
Tries someone else.
Nothing.
And another.
Nope.
It's like she can't be alone with her mind.
Her hands are tiny.
Neck too.
All of her.
At last she gets through only her tone softens and she talks about something else.
"Alright mum got me those trainers? ... why you said you would ... well get them then I need them for the weekend cos I'm going out ... just get them yeah ... alright, yeah ... just don't get pink ... don't get me pink whatever you do ... pink, NO! Well use ya head you know what I like ... not pink and don't get nuffin chavified or nuffin ... yeah, alright ... I'm on the bus ... I don't know...bout half hour ... yeah ... ya are gonna get em aren't ya? Well go online then ... I swear mum I need them for the weekend uvverwise I can't go ... fuck off I'm not wearing *them* ... cos they're fuckin old man ... ancient ... just get em mum please ... not pink and not chavified or nuffin...alright bye."

She tries ringing someone else when I notice this fat Chinese woman across from her.

Trouble, I think.

"Yo Marcia guess which fuckin bitch just tried frontin me at da bus stop yeah."

Chinese snaps.

On her feet.

Leaning over the girl.

"We do not *all* want to hear your filthy mouth."

Girl is startled for about half a second.

Then rage takes over.

"Who the fuck ya talking too. Get out my face, yeah!"

Chinese sits but doesn't back-down.

"Your language is disgusting and this is a public place."

"Here, here!" someone shouts from the front.

One person claps.

Then another.

Girl looks shocked.

Like she didn't realise how loud she was.

Face flushes.

Embarrassment and rage.

50/50.

She flies off the handle.

Starts screaming.

I catch the eyes of the driver in the rear-view.

A few other people have joined in on the girl.

Think it's time I made my cameo.

I fix my hair, a little.

Pull the t-shirt around my frame.

Breathe.

Stand.

Here I am.

On scene.

Enter me:

"Why don't you all leave the little daisy-chain alone?"

My voice is no way near as loud as the others but for some reason it finds its way through and silences the crowd.

Even girl.

All eyes on me.

As usual.

I look one way.

Then the other.

Realise I'm wearing sunglasses so I take them off, slowly.

"Granted. Our girl doesn't possess much etiquette in the linguistic department but we should be looking after her."

I walk the bus.

Slide in next to her.

And sit.

Definitely Jack Nicholson.

More *Easy Rider* this time.

"What ya doin?" she says, sheepish.

I ignore.

Turn my attention to the others.

"Go on. *Sit*. Drama over. You can all go back to your private worlds."

They do.

I carry on looking ahead.

The girl is staring at me.

"What ya doin?" she says again.

"Do you have any idea how magic you are?"

I look at her for the first time.

Right in the eyes.

Her expression is everywhere.

Her mouth tries to find a word.

But fails.

"You're going to be alright," I say.

"Are you a perv or somethin?" she says nervously. "And what do you mean magic?"

Her voice is tiny.

Like her hands.

And neck.

"Do me a favour," I say.

Pause.

"Go home and look in the mirror. Don't talk to your mum. Don't talk to anybody. Don't worry about pink trainers or girls at the bus stop or any of that shit. Turn that phone off and keep it turned off and just look in the mirror and you'll know what I'm talking about."

Her face has changed, *completely*.

"Will you do that for me?"

She nods, slowly.

The bus goes silent.

Even the babies have stopped crying and the people who get on are quiet too, like they can *sense* something.
Two stops later she rings the bell.
I let her out.
Our hands touch.
I watch her through the window.
Standing still on the pavement.
She's smiling.
Or maybe smiling.
Just.

Not frowning.

Strawberry Letter

I sit with you on the beach. You are asleep and I do my best to take care of you. Make sure the sun doesn't burn you. Watch out for the tide. Keep away the insects. And the other men. My toes are warm in the sand. I lick an ice cream and watch the boats bob on the horizon. When you wake I go buy us a punnet of strawberries. They are cool. Sweet. Delicious. We eat them one by one. Until they are gone. Until there is none.

Boy

Feel like Christian Slater.

Slater in his prime.
True Romance.
Wayward, wacky and wistful.
Hawaiian shirt.
I sit at the back of the bus, next to the fire exit.
Two stops later a boy gets on.
Hear him before I see him.
"He's a lickle pussy-ole man," he fires into his phone.
I lean in and take a closer look.
Small.
Tracksuit.
Big, white trainers.
Lively.
Wiry.
A live wire.
"*Nah,* if I see him again the lickle faggit is getting smashed-up, *proper.*"
The word 'faggit' grabs the attention of the man opposite, who raises his head in an instant.
Tension grips the bus and I notice movement from all the rest who are sat here.
Some stare out the window.
Others look down.
Someone puts their earphones in.
"Kyle yeah, I'm not even joking, *yeah.* You see dat lickle batty-boy yeah ya smash him up, proper."
"Excuse me."
Trouble, I think.
The man opposite has spoken only Boy is lost in his world. "He don't roll like us man ... he is a lickle faggit-batty-boy who is gonna get smashed."
Man snaps.
On his feet.
"We do not *all* want to hear your filthy mouth."
Boy is startled for about half a second.
Then rage takes over.

"Who the fuck ya talking to …" Then into his phone. "Yo let me ring ya back cah this pussy-ole on the bus is about to get smashed-up."

Man sits but doesn't back-down.

"Your language is disgusting and this is a public place."

"Here, here!" someone shouts from the front.

One person claps.

Then another.

His face screws-up and snarls, "yo what ya *all* clapping for?!"

He goes over the edge.

Starts screaming.

I catch the eyes of the driver in the rear-view.

"All of ya, come-on!"

His arms spread-eagle the width of the bus, offering us all out.

People gasp, quake.

For a moment I picture him cracking the man.

It's so close I can see it, feel it.

The bus pulls up and the driver shouts something but it's smothered as Boy goes ballistic, "Come step to me solo."

Boy now reaches into his pocket and the gasps turn to cries, one person sobbing.

Offended Man is now white and regret sets deep in his nonplussed expression.

Driver has opened his door but someone screams "NO" so he closes it.

"Call the police," someone says.

"That won't be necessary."

It's me. I have spoken.

Boy's eyes shrink to tiny dots as he tries to work out who the voice belongs to.

His head ducking and weaving.

"Don't!" A horrified voice says.

"Just call the – "

His eyes meet mine for the first time, as I float up the bus.

Towards him.

"It's okay brother. It's okay, *son*."

"What?!"

"I know."

"Fuck … you … say?"

He's confused of a sudden.

"I know."

"Know what?!!"

"Forget these idiots," I say.

"Yo, yo! Ya better back the fuck – "

"Forget them *all*."

"Yo."

"I'm not coming any closer," I say, moving closer. "I've been here the whole time."

Now his face is really confused and really pale and I'm almost by his side, within touching distance.

"All your life."

"What?"

He tries to rage again but a slow hand guides it back down.

"It's okay."

"No it's not," he whimpers now.

"Oh but it is."

I'm next to him, by his side for real.

"Do you think these people can possibly understand your obscurity."

"What?"

"Do you think these people can possibly know what you've been through."

A woman now, with a strong clear voice speaks up. "Excuse me but I'm not buying this crap. I've been through stuff too, we *all* have. It doesn't give him the right to – "

Boy tenses up again, fire relit.

"Forget these fools," I say. "It's just me."

"Pussy-ole. FUCK."

"I'm the only one who counts."

Boy finds his pocket again and a single scream cuts through the bus.

"Son, *boy*. It's alright, man."

I look at the talking woman.

"Just let him work it," someone says at the back.

The woman shakes her head and goes back to the window.

"Come sit with me." I say to the boy. "Come sit."

"You don't know me man!"

"I know."

"About 'they don't know what you've been through,' *you don't know me*."

"I know."

He gets younger by the second, 17, 15, 13, 9.

"C'mon boy," I say.

"You ... don't ... know ... *me*."

I say nothing more.

Just stroll back up the bus and somehow he follows.

And somehow the bus starts up and begins to move.

Pulls away and moves and as it passes through a short dark tunnel a silence falls over us all like a blanket.

Almost peaceful, maybe hypnotic.

I expect people to get off but they don't.

I expect people to get on but they don't.

There's just this strange, soundless autopilot to everything.

The boy has his head down the whole time and I feel how exhausted he is.

How exhausted we all are.

Two stops later I ring the bell.

He lets me out.

I hold out a Big Fist and he bumps it but won't give me any eye-contact.

Standing on the pavement I watch him through the window.

His head down and smiling.

Or maybe not smiling.

Just.

Not frowning.

Blondes

You're trying to read *this* sentence only you're distracted by two blonde dots hovering over the page. The image hurts your eyes. It's as if two blazing suns have suddenly appeared in the dull, grey sky. You put the book down and inch tentatively down the grass bank you're lounging on. If you listen carefully, very carefully, you can just about hear their voices at the bus stop.

    JENNA: Hey.
    MYRA: Hello.
    JENNA: What are we doing here?
    MYRA: Waiting for a bus.
    JENNA: Hey I've seen your face somewhere before. Are you like famous or something?
    MYRA: Kind of.
    JENNA: What do you do?
    MYRA: Well, uh, I'm an archaeologist. I'm trying to find some buried treasure so they can like me again.
    JENNA: Cool.
    MYRA: Hm.
    JENNA: I'm famous too. Or going to be at least. I'm the princess of the adult entertainment industry.
    MYRA: Pornography?
    JENNA: I'm only 19.
    MYRA: Nobody looks like you. You're not real.
    JENNA: Thanks.
    MYRA: I'm not real either. Not anymore. I'm just a name that hangs in people's minds.
    JENNA: Hey we're both blonde! You could be my mom. I've never had a mom before. People say that's why I entered the industry. Because I had no mom. They say it's a psychology thing.
    MYRA: Well, uh, I'm not a real blonde. And I don't think I should be your mum either. People say I'm not very good with children.
    JENNA: I wouldn't worry about what people say. I think you'd be a great mom. As for the blonde I wouldn't worry about that either. Your hair is amazing. I've never seen anything like it. What style is that?

MYRA: Beehive.
JENNA: Can I touch it?
MYRA: Just the once.

Deleted Scene

Saw the prostitute in the supermarket.

Hooker in the store.
Had her head down.
Or maybe not.
But there was an air of self-consciousness about her.
Like she was aware.
Of who she was and what she did.
Of the people who *could* know.
Like a famous person trying to avoid attention.
I know how she feels.
Anyway.
What little of her face I did see was caked in make-up.
Make-up that had been there for a while.
Days.
Make-up that made her face tired.
Ache.
Her tall, good figure.
But nobody would know.
I did.
I was there, man.
At the self-serving check-out.
I couldn't believe she was buying a whole chicken.
Couldn't imagine her as a hostess.
Couldn't imagine her as anything other than what she was.
I slowed the packing of my own bags so we could leave at the same time.
"Hi," I said.
We both had the sun on us.
When I saw her eyes I thought of beetles.
She was already walking away, fast.
"You don't remember me do you?"
"Fuck off!" she spat.
She seemed more like a hooker now, hips swaying.
"But I gave you a nice massage. You fell asleep in my arms."
She stopped suddenly and stepped forward.
Looked hard at me, trying to work me out.
After a while she gave up and turned away sharp on her heels.

She didn't remember me.
She didn't remember me at all.

Our time together just wasn't memorable enough for her.

Muhammad Ali

On his eleventh birthday Joe Cassius met Muhammad Ali. It was a book signing event and the queue ran all the way through the centre of town. Lil Joe and his mum sat at the back of the bus and watched this bow of people stretch for a mile long.

The little boy's mother began having second thoughts.

"Oh Joe this is silly, we'll be here all day."

Even at that age he knew this was a once in a lifetime thing. Even though Lil Joe was a shy boy he was determined. She wasn't getting out of it. She was just going to have to wait.

She was right, though. They did stand in it all day. By the end it was dark and they were so tired they couldn't feel their feet anymore.

As they got near the front news broke: because of his Parkinson's he wasn't signing any autographs today. Instead they had to buy his book with an already-made signature inside. If you didn't buy the book then you didn't get to meet him.

In short, a scam.

Mum was furious.

She was *this close* from stepping out the queue and going home. Again Lil Joe was determined. He had to remind her that this was a once in a lifetime thing. He also had to remind her what this man had done for black people all over the world and that as a black family this had the significance of a pilgrimage.

"You're eleven years old," his mum smiled. "How do you get to talk like that?"

"Besides, we've been in this queue all day," Lil Joe said. "Leaving it now would be stupid. And, it's my birthday. I'll never forgive you."

He stressed the word never, *never*.

In the end his mother got the picture.

Not far to go and an old man approached them from the street. He looked sad. He told them that he too had queued all day but because he couldn't afford to buy the book they had turned him away. In his hand was a programme of when Ali fought Joe Bugner in 1975.

"My name is Joe too!" Lil Joe said.

The old man asked if he could pretend he was with them so at least he could go in and meet him. Joe's mum was suspicious of white people and the little boy had to pull her sleeve.

In the end she was so tired she just nodded her head.

At last they got to the door. Lil Joe had been holding in a pee for the last three hours.

The security guards were massive and it was the first time he heard a real-life American voice. It was directed at the old man who was pretending to be his grandad.

"You can go in and meet him sir but do not ask him to sign that there programme."

The sight of The Greatest rendered Joe's white grandpa speechless. He went even whiter and couldn't move for a moment or two. They let him go first. He shuffled over and shook his hand. Said a few words. It was then that The Greatest took the programme from his hand and signed it. His hands were shaking all over the place because of the Parkinson's but he did it. When he gave it him back the old man broke down and cried.

Now it was Lil Joe's turn. His shyness went away and he ran at the giant and flung his arms around him, kissed his big handsome face before sitting on his lap like Father Christmas.

"Can I ask you something?" he said.

Muhammad Ali looked down at the child.

"Why did you change your name? The first one was much cooler."

He let out a deep, lovable chuckle.

Then,

His eyes went really big and he said in a soft slur. "You like it so much son…you can have it."

A Dream I Had About A Fox

Out at night.

   Again.
   Walking a country lane.
   There is something in the road.
   A bump.
   A lump of something.
   The one bit of light holds it in its glare.
   I stand over it.
   Can't believe the size of it.
   The *sheer volume* of the thing.
   At first I think it's a dog.
   Or, as crazy as this sounds, a wolf.
   It is a fox.
   A dead fox.
   Foxes to me are small, speedy things.
   Stationary makes them bigger.
   I bend over and look at it.
   Wind makes its face move.
   Is it dead?
   Get closer.
   My shadow slips over it.
   It is mangled.
   Ripped apart.
   One whole side is torn off.
   It's open.
   I can see *inside*.
   All kinds of things are there.
   Organs and veins and tubes and bubbles and bones.
   I see *everything*.
   I walk around and look at it from all angles.
   Its teeth are showing.
   It was scared.
   Its eye is mad.
   Yellow.
   Intimate.
   Its eye screams at me.
   It stares and I stare back.

A contest.
Who will look away first?
The blood looks like paint.
Swirls of pink and red and bits of black.
I look at it for so long that it loses the word *fox*.
It becomes something else.
Like a squished birthday cake.
I bend down further and touch it.
A paw.
A tooth.
The tongue.
Not the eye though.
Leave *that* alone.
Put my hand *inside* and feel for the heart.
Finger half a dozen things and anyone of them could be the heart.
Still the eye looks at me.
Always.
Get tired so decide to head home.
As I leave I hear the sound of a car.
Headlights light up the road.
Creep into a bush.
And watch.
The vehicle runs over the fox.
Imagine the people in the car.
What they would say.
"Did you see that?"
"Gross."
I want to go back and see how the fox will have changed shape only I'm too tired.
Tomorrow, I think.
When I get home I see my mum there.
Standing at the sink.
Washing pots.
She's like me, I'd think.
Always of the night.
"Did you have a good evening, son?"
"Ah, just went bowling with some friends."
She'd smile.
"There's apple pie in the fridge."

I'd put the pie on the table and begin to eat it with my bloody fingers.

"Oh son, wash your hands at least."

Letter

Seing as tho you ACTUALLY think my hand-writting is cute then i'm sending you this insted of a prtined one. HA. MAN. what a year and hear we are back agen not back how we were but how we are and a new improvd version. Id like to think. A deeper, higher levul of spiritual conection. US. So happy I git rid of that twat but not talkin bout him in this. This is about US. Ure back in my life with all the fredum we want. wowwowwow. can you beleev I was so nervous bout nocking on your door that day after over a year even tho u thought it was only a few monthes. NO SENSE OF TIME. Ha. When you ACTUALLY openned up and I saw you handsum face all the absense and hart ache and missing-you-stuff just varnished away and we were write back ware we were like nuhtin had changed and you were the same in a diffrent way of you eating biskits and making me laf and not giveing a fuck and it was just amazing and who was I kiding to be going out with boringben and his jelus ways. Thankyou for listing and holding me like you used to. And all ways did. Felt good to be in your arms agen. And you no what im not even botherred about your new girlfriend even tho you say shes not your gf becarse you dont do titles mr fredum but you cant hide from me mr sociopath I can see the love in your eyes becarse ive seen the same look you once had for me you think I forget. HA!! Tho tbh I was kindof suprized almost shocked and kindof jelus but ben showed me what jelusy looks like and its not very ugly. Is one ugly muthafucka is jelusy so im not haveing it in my life. yuk! Nuthin gud can never come form jelusy. uther "bad" emotions hav benefits. rage can make u feel alive, sadnes can make you longing and dealth can bee reflectiev, and even frusraion can leed to creative things but jelsuy is nuthin but orrfullness. like its a road too no ware and you just go rownd in circuls.
SO . . . . i LIKE CLOE! I except her and love her and IM AS sure she is as luvly and misteroius as you say. Wow u with anutther girl But shes in our life and does she rarely not talk!!!?????? You go form one xtream to the other. Wot wiht me meing a motormouth. Ha. Love its all about love there shud be no barriers or boxes and that's wot I luv about us.

Any way. Glad ur back. And I get to kiss ur face and sniff your armpitts agen. Wonderful!

You are my handsum rouge"
My incurabel death boy.
ILOVEYOU.
Amber (yes I can spell my own name. your dyslexia queen.
PS. I purfosely didn't hold back on this letter and this writing and didn't give a fuck about the speelling and just let rip becarse I no you think my handwriting and spelling is cute. Plus my councellor said I juys just not hold back alet it all outso this is me <u>pure!!</u>

Pps<u> and I always right to you when my meds are werking and i'm on the</u> 'up.'
<u>*Makes me swing through the trees. Uber Creative!*</u>

Like Salvdor Dali, Virginya Wolf and Mick Jagger haveing a threesum. HA

Any way.
I'm going now.

A x

Cattchya later Monster Man

She's Like The Wind

In bed.

    Can't sleep.
    But.
    Can't be bothered to go out.
    Imagination runs wild.
    Chloe is in *here*.
    We're laying in the long grass.
    Sun out.
    Birds, too.
    They tweet
    A song comes on.
    Just for us.
    The man himself.
    Swayze.
    That intro.
    Piano.
    Sax.
    She's Like The Wind.
    We're both wearing white.
    Chloe and I.
    Fringe shading her eyes.
    Short skirt.
    Looking at her calf.
    Her calf looking back.
    "You know this ain't real?" she says.
    Look at her face.
"I would never talk like this and I wouldn't be listening to this song and I definitely wouldn't be wearing this hideous skirt. This is *all* your imagination."

"I know." I say, cup of my hand a millimetre away from her calf. "But isn't everything?"

Joe Cassius

Saw Joe Cassius. Same second-hand bookshop. Reading one of his own books again.

"This is a nasty habit you're developing," I said.

Made him jump. Made him turn red.

"Oh god," he said.

We laughed. Noticed he was wearing one of those *Teenage Mutant Ninja Turtles* badges again. This time the red one, Raphael. He's the emotional one who kicks off all the time. Again I was going to ask him about it but again we got talking about something else. Got talking about writing and the writing process and how it works. How it works for him.

"I write things down on scraps of paper," he said. "Then transfer them into a notebook. Then type up."

"Why not just write directly into the pad?" I asked.

"Don't like carrying it around. Terrified in case I lose it. I keep it at home. Where it's safe."

"What if you get burgled?"

He smiled that big Caribbean smile. Knew I was putting him on.

I asked him if he was working on anything now and he told me he's been working on *this* novel. I asked him what it's about and he told me that he's not quite sure. I asked him what the title was and he told me that he's not sure about that either.

"It's between three," he said.

"Tell me the three," I said.

"Okay."

He was perspiring. His ebony skin glistened.

"The candidates are: *This Weirdish Wild Space, Chloe's Calf,* or, *A Happy Orphan*."

I pulled a face, then smiled.

"Got to be the third," I said.

"Why?"

"Well I've just recently become an orphan myself."

"Oh. I'm sorry to hear that," he said, genuinely sad.

"But," I went on. "I'm back on that horse and surviving. Happy. Guess you could say I'm A Happy Orphan."

Joe Cassius shook my hand, "thank you young man. Think you've just made my decision for me. Think I have the title to my new novel. And I'm dedicating it to you."

"No," I said. "Dedicate it to *us*."

"Done," he said.

I felt happy and was about to ask if he wanted to celebrate and go for a drink. But then I remembered that Joe Cassius was a very private man.

A Happy Orphan

Joe Cassius

Dedicated to Us

"What's powerful about a love scene is not seeing the act. It's seeing the passion, the need, the desire, the caring, the fear."

Patrick Swayze

Kurt Cobain

I remember our first kiss. We were fifteen. You could have been sixteen. We had walked home from school and were hanging-out on your porch. As always. Only there was something different about it this time. Something in the air. Maybe it was nerves. You were nervous and I was nervous. It was April the 5th. I remember because it was the day Kurt Cobain died. Only we didn't know yet because of the Atlantic Time Difference. You always said I looked like Kurt. Or some kind of rock star, at least. It had been raining and rainwater collected on the canopy of the fishing boat in the driveway. We talked for hours. Until it was dark. You were waiting for me to make my move but I was scared. Your mum came out and told us off. Told us to get inside because she could *hear our stomachs rumbling from here.* I wanted to come inside but I could tell you didn't want me to. It was written all over your face. When she went back in you stepped into me. Remember the scent of you. And the very words you said.

"You're the only one who makes sense."

My hands instinctively found your waist. Then we kissed. You were my first and I think I was yours. Or maybe second. I closed my eyes and remembered how they did it in the movies. All of it was great. I'd define it as The Perfect First Kiss. In the end a cat jumped up the fence and startled us and our bodies went into shock like we'd been hit by a bolt of lightning.

O.J. Simpson and Rosanna Arquette at Miami Beach

My mother and I are sitting in the hospital where she is now a permanent resident. It is a cottage-like building at the edge of the south entrance, away from the main block. It is situated between two big tress and it is most pleasant. I have two Bret Easton Ellis novels with me, which I read while one of the nurses gets her ready and puts her back in bed. She has her sunglasses on and keeps touching her hair and I keep looking at my hands, pretty sure they're shaking. She tries to smile when she asks me what I want for Christmas. I'm surprised at how much effort it takes to raise my head and look at her.

"Nothing," I say.

There's a tea-sipping pause and then I say, "what do you want?"

She says nothing for a long time and I look back at my hands, which are now glistening in the morning sun. My mother folds her lips inwards, and says, "I don't know. I just want to have a nice Christmas."

I don't say anything.

"You look unhappy," she says real suddenly.

"I'm never unhappy," I tell her.

"I've been here before," she says, all far-off. "Like a déjà vu. I've been here *twice* before."

She touches her pitch-black Japanese hair and I look down at the two Ellis novels, facing up from the wicker chair to my right.

"You look unhappy," she says, more quietly and profoundly this time.

"Well, you do too," I say slowly, hoping she won't say anything else.

She doesn't say anything else. I move to another chair by the window, and through the bars the lawn darkens outside. My whole life I've lived in America. Not real America but the one in my head. I look further to see a vague city skyline with a backdrop of the ocean.

"How was the party?" she asks.

"Okay," I say, guessing.

"How many people were there?"

"Forty. Fifty." I shrug.

Just then I notice the black man walk in. He nods his head sadly at us and then shuffles forwards towards his wife opposite. I honestly don't know how his wife is still alive. She looks dead, *literally* dead. She's like a flat white sack of bones, veins, teeth and eyeballs. The husband takes a seat by her bed and kisses her forehead, "hello my darling."

I look at my mum, and her eyes water up and glisten in the late afternoon light.

I've been here all day. All the relatives are here all day and all night.

Eventually the wife falls back to sleep and then the husband does too. He looks so old and broken. While they sleep and my mum sleeps I get up and look at the photo on their bedside table. It is the couple in their early-thirties. They are stupidly attractive in the 1980's. He looks like O.J. Simpson and she looks like Rosanna Arquette, dead ringers. They are standing and smiling fearlessly and joyously at the camera. Further behind them there is a vague city skyline with a backdrop of the ocean.

Book Shop

You first saw me in the book shop, remember? You came in and clocked me standing against the back wall. Maybe you saw the others first. But then you saw me and walked over. Intrigued but a little unsure. Your hand touched me. Felt your fingers, then thumb. Your grip was tight. Kind of made me lose my breath. You picked me up and took me down. Turned me over. The others watched on. A little jealous. Hoping you would put me back and pick them. You didn't. I could tell I was the one. I had you. You had me. We were hooked. I knew from that moment it was going to work. That we were going to be good for each other. You weren't interested in the others. I had your attention and held it there, *here*. We stood looking at each other. Seemed for ages. Still in your hands. You seemed to be swaying, like we were dancing. I wanted you to do something dangerous. *Steal me*. Pop me in your pocket or drop me into a shopping bag. Nobody was watching. Nobody was there. Just that old lady in the romance section and the geeks in sci-fi. You could have gotten away with it, easy. But. You didn't. Instead you took me to the counter and paid for me. Swiped your plastic and stamped your loyalty card and that was it. I was yours. All yours. You took me to the coffee shop and pulled me out and opened me up and you haven't stopped since.

Megan

is doing well with her eating. She's doing a lot of it now and seems to be on the right track with her mission.

"I have targets," she says.

She's doing well with her weight. She's banged loads of it on. Four stone in just as many months. I think. Obviously it's all down to diet. Diet is key. Last night she ate three chocolate gateaus, one after the other while watching the *Back to the Future* trilogy. I watched her do it.

"Right now I'm obese. Another stone and I'll qualify as *morbidly* obese. I want to be morbid. Morbid is what I'm aiming for."

On the table next to us is a photo of her in a bikini. She was nineteen when this was taken. It's when she used to work as a stripper. She won a contest once called: Hot Bod Babe Fest.

"I was a champion. But now I want to head in the opposite direction. *Wrong direction.* Or what people *believe* is the wrong direction. I want to get rid of what people think is good. It's about choice. Self-sabotage. Maybe it's a Jesus thing. A religion thing. I want to prove that happiness is what's on the *in*side. Not the *out*. To be honest I don't quite know what I'm doing. It just *feels* right."

The thing she eats most is pasta. She eats tones of it. Anelloni. Barbina. Bigoli. Bucanti. Capelli d'angelo. Capellini. Fedelini. Fusilli. Fusilli bucati. Maccheroni alla molinera. Matriciani. Perciatelli. Pici. Spaghetti. Spaghettini. Spaghettoni. Vermicelli. Vermicelloni. Ziti. Zitoni.

Also: Linguine. Scialatelli. Cannelloni. Ditalini. Paccheri. Gemelli. Lasange. Rotini. Tagiatelle. And Stringozzi. There could be more. I gave her this idea from Robert De Niro. This is what he did to gain weight for the film *Raging Bull.*

"People say I look like De Niro," I say.

"You don't."

"Pacino then?"

We sit on the sofa and eat biscuits. There's rolls under her shirt. Rolls and rolls. She's a wide load, from hip to hip. Face big, wedged between a sharp, square bob.

"What do your parents think to all this?"

"All what?"

"Getting fat. Getting big. You know, your mission?"

"My mish?"
"Yeah."
"They don't get it. They think it's a lesbian thing."

Nicholas Elliot

"See you're reading *A Happy Orphan*?"

His voice startles you from the bushes. A man from the blue. This wino meditating on a wall with a bag of booze by his feet.

You stop, "pardon?"

He throws his head back and a mop of blonde hair follows it. "The book peeking out of your pocket."

"Oh," you say, looking down. "Yeah I'm reading *A Happy Orphan*."

The man looks at you with crazy, beautiful eyes of blue. He smiles and then tries to hold down some regurgitated alcohol in this throat.

"Did you know that one day that book in your pocket is going to be scientifically proven as the 93rd greatest novel of all-time?"

This makes you laugh out-loud. "What?"

"Tis true. I know cos I've seen in. I've been there."

He smiles again and you see a chipped tooth which brings more handsome magic to his face.

"You've been to the future?" You say, eyebrows arched.

"Oh sure," he says, launching an empty can over his shoulder. His hand plunges into the plastic, plucking out another. Pulls at the ring-pull. Crack. Hiss. Slurp. Sip.

"Want one?"

Part of you is repulsed, part of you is tempted. "Nah," You say. "Bit early."

"Early is best," he says. "I drink for the hangover."

"What?"

"I drink to get back up. This is where I get my visions."

You take a quick look around you. People going to work. People at the bus stop. People walking their dogs. It's like no one notices him on the wall. And because you're talking to him it's like they don't notice you either. It's like he's made you invisible, taken you into another dimension.

"Visions?" You say, re-entering the conversation.

"One of them is in that book you're reading."

Now you know he is mad. "What?"

"See for yourself," he says, tipping his head back, one eye open; sun winking off the can.

You think about walking on, leaving this nut to his nuttiness.

"Page eighty-nine" he says casually.

You're still smiling, shaking your head. The pages of this book skim past your thumb as you flick through for 89.

Go on, look ...

... found it ...

"A piece of dust goes a long way," You mutter, reading from the page, "It's an old story."

"It's about time."

"What?"

"And space."

"I ..."

"Wrote it during one of my visions."

"You're Nicholas Elliot?"

"Actually I didn't write it. I just thunk it."

"Oh c'mon," You say, amused.

"Joe Cassius wrote it. I just gave him permission to put it *here*."

"You expect me to believe this?"

Nicholas Elliot finishes another can of alcohol.

"You have to believe me. It's in the sentence above, *look*."

"What?"

"My name in black and white."

You look at his name in black and white, then at his face. His eyes are smiling their head off.

"You look like you need a drink," he says, handing you a can.

This time you take it and sit next to him. "Drink with me and you'll see the same things I see," he says. "You'll have visions."

You both see a ladybird hover through space. An old man limping down the street. A bus pulls up, two blondes get on. A boy delivering papers. Someone's voice behind you, complaining about the beer cans piling up in their garden.

Diary of A Sexy Bastard

Today.

    I wake somewhere around 10:30.
    Lay here for a while.
    Listening:
    Siren.
    Breeze blowing the fence.
    Music from four doors down.
    Humming through the walls.
    Mind feels exceptionally clean.
    Body strong.
    Tan.
    Smooth.
    Hard.
    Not a speck of fat.
    Everything feels *streamlined.*
    Lean over and take a sip of Evian.
    Pick up a new book that my friend Nicholas Elliot gave me.
    A Happy Orphan by Joe Cassius.
    Gotta say it's some impressive shit.
    Genius in fact.
    The black boy can write, there's no doubt about it.
    Up there with the top lads, for sure.
    What makes it great is the pure humility of the man.
    Cassius is a very humble human being.
    A rare one.
    I could learn a lot from him.
    After chapter **69** I put the book down and stare out the window, in awe.
    Wow, what a mind, I think.
    Back to reality.
    Check my phone.
    Texts from Amber and Ben.

Baby let's do lunch, my treat! X

Bastard I'm gonna kill you!

Bet you can guess which text is from whom.
I head to the kitchen and fix a little breakfast.
Bowl of muesli washed down with a glass of orange juice.
Then a single poached egg.
Small cup of black coffee.
Hit gym.
Several girls turn at the treadmills to watch me enter.
I'm only 5ft2 today but I'm like a little Sly Stallone with the face of Paul Newman.
Fucking ridiculous.
Like I said at the beginning, *offensive*.
It's almost unfair and a twinge of guilt pricks my guts as I pick up a dumbbell and stand next to *the other men*.
Ben.
Poor fucker never had a chance.
Wonder what he's doing *now*.
Probably still in bed.
Wanking and eating himself to death.
I need to help him.
Heal him.
It's my duty.
Black girl and white girl look at me to look to them but all I can think about is Chloe.
Her calf can't be long now, surely.
Our date with destiny is nigh.
I hit the mat and start my crunch set.
When a big, aggressive alpha-type starts doing some on the mat next to me.
He sits facing the other way.
We sit-up in sync.
His face is forward, focussed,
After about 20 crunches I say, cheerily,
"Hey dude we're in 69!"
He blinks.
Flash of shock across his face.
Not sure if he's heard me right yet he's too uncomfortable to ask.
After gym I hit Amber with a reply to her text.

Lunch. Sure.

First I swing-by Sun Showers and ray-up, top-up.

"You look well."
Amber says as we take seat at an *al fresco* café.
I sit with my eyes closed and the sun on my face.
"What are you doing?" she says.
Pause .... "enjoying the mind."
Open my eyes and look at Amber.
She's confused.
I stretch: "Ahhhh ... don't you ever have those days," I say. "When you look around at the world and the people in it and think that every human being is just so fucking gorgeous! I mean look at them all."
I wave a hand across them.
"Fucking beautiful."
Amber looks spaced-out.
Must be the meds.
The waitress brings our food.
"Cheers baby."
She looks at me, offended.
I wink.
Amber's face is amber.
"Ben isn't so beautiful," she says.
I pick up some food and put it in my mouth, "sure he is."
"No. He's not."
"I like his voice. Something fragile and endearing to his voice. I'd like to cuddle it."
Amber's eyes are big.
Must be the meds.
"You want to cuddle his voice?"
"Yeah I want to cuddle his voice."
"You know he wants to kill you."
I wave her off. "Nah, that's just how he *feels*."
"People *are* what they feel," she says.
"What?"
She says my name. Then, "you really don't understand people do you?"
I stare at the waitress's calf.
Now I know why I adore Chloe's so much.
All the others in the world just simply don't compare.

Amber clicks her fingers in front of my face and breaks my daydream.

"Ben!"

"What?"

"We were talking about Ben. He's starting to scare me."

"Why?"

"He's drinking too much and acting weird. He's even lost his job."

"I know how he feels."

"What?"

"Where did he lose it?"

"In the storm."

"He'll get another one."

We eat.

"Did you give him…a say?" I say, mouth full.

"A what?"

"A say. Like I say. You need to give him *a say*."

Amber makes a noise through her straw. "Don't start that again."

"Every man needs a say."

"I've blocked him. You should too. Why do you even take his calls?"

"I can't give up on him yet."

"I don't even know why I bother asking you anything."

"Wisdom."

"What?"

"Wiz."

"You're round the fucking bend."

"Hey. You're on medication. I drink a pot of tea."

I say, holding up my milkshake.

"What!"

"You know what I'm talking about."

Amber looks at me, hate and lust in her eyes at the same time.

"All I'm saying is that Ben will be okay, *in the end*. He and I are probably more similar than you think. We might even have the same soul, just different bodies."

Amber looks into the sky.

Think she gets what I mean.

I start to suck on my milkshake.

Hard.

Eyes wide.

Cheeks disappeared.

Aiming to drain in one blast.
That gratifying suction sound at the bottom.
"He told me he's been carrying a knife."
I put the glass down and put my head in my hands.
"You alright?" she says. "Has that scared you?"
"I sucked too hard. Too much passion. Brain-freeze headache. Shake-ache, I call it. It's alright. It'll pass in a minute."
Amber shakes her head.
From nowhere an almighty gust of wind hits us.
Rattles the tables.
People laugh.
Scream.
Try and hold things down.
Commotion.
"God's just burped," I say.
Everyone is amused by that.
"You don't believe in God," Amber says.
"Sure I do," I reply, catching my reflection in the window.
We finish up and pay up.
We spend the rest of the day together.
Walk in the park.
Cinema.
Another meal out.
At night we lay in bed.
She's always the same, head hits the pillow and gone.
Must be the meds.
I lay here in the dark.
After a few hours I start to drop, fall.
From nowhere I feel a stab of pain and I know Ben is out there.
Somewhere.
In the dark.
Thinking about me.
And I know this.

Because I am thinking about him.

Dude's Fucking-Up

You imagine what Ben is doing today. He'll wake somewhere around 10:30. His first thought will be *Amber*. Her image will split through his head and open his day. *She* will be where it all starts. He still can't believe she's gone. He'll be hung-over. Not a big hangover. But an annoying little one. They'll be a headache. Dry-mouth. They'll be no work to go to. He'll either be laid-off or on sick or just not turned up. He'll be worried about it. On his mind. One of the many things on his mind. He won't be able to get out of bed. Won't need to. Because everything is right *here*. On tap. He's built himself *a depressive's cave*. Two bottles by his bed. One to drink from and the other to piss in. He drinks cheap, flat cola. Gets a sugar rush. His teeth are furry and a blister-capped ulcer throbs under his tongue. He'll eat from a giant bag of Doritos. Before flipping on the TV with remote control. *Jeremy Kyle*. He watches people scream at each other. He used to find this amusing. Now he just gazes into it like a zombie. Something reminds him to check his phone so he does. Nothing in the inbox but plenty in the out. Mostly to Amber and Our Hero.

Can't live without you!! X

I'm gonna kill you!!

You can guess which text is to whom. He'll finish the Doritos and now his mouth is dusty and yellow. *Jeremy Kyle* ends and *This Morning* begins. He'll watch Holly Willoughby and burn with desire. She knocks Amber to the back of his mind, *for now*. He's in love with Holly. Thinks she's *angelic*. He's in lust with Holly too. Thinks she's *juicy*. A hand creeps into the crusty depths of his underwear. Only she's interviewing a blind woman and every time he's about to climax either the blind woman or her guide dog come on the screen. In the end he closes his eyes and remembers Amber only it hurts too much and he loses his erection. He feels inadequate and heartbroken and ends up crying into his pillow. He cries so much it makes him exhausted so he falls back to sleep. He dreams. He dreams about him, Our Hero. Has a dream about you. He doesn't know what he looks like so his mind makes him into a black, featureless man hovering over his world. *Omnipresent.*

Following him down nameless streets. Slipping in and out of his head at random times. Just like in Real Life. He wakes with hatred and picks up his phone and rings him only there is no answer this time. Instead he looks in the mirror and a man looks back. His teeth are bad. His whole appearance says *neglect*. This is what love does. He's pale and dark-eyed. A scruffy beard housing Dorito-droppings. He's fat and thin at the same time. He wants to scream out-loud but his mum might be downstairs and he doesn't want to upset her *even more*. This is what love does. So, he'll get out of this bed, *eventually*. Puts his hood up and goes outside. *It's not dark yet, but it's getting there.* Goes to the nearest off-license and buys three cans of cider. Hits the park and sits on a swing. Up and down while sipping. After the second can he'll start to feel better. Remembers some of the advice you once gave him and for the first time ever there is a feeling of fondness towards me. It's fleeting. Within a few seconds he goes back to the hating of me. The cans are gone so he'll head to the nearest pub. He'll sit next to an old woman in the corner. They'll drink together until closing and then go back to her house. They'll take their clothes off and pass the bottle back and forth until they pass out. He'll wake three hours later and not have a clue where he is. In a room all alone. Just a picture on the wall of an old woman and a fat kid. He'll leave. Outside he recognises where he is. Apple Tree Lane. As he walks something sticks in his leg. He reaches inside his pocket to find a kitchen knife. Must have stolen it, he thinks. He begins to talk to the knife. He gives it a name and says it has a purpose. The knife is a girl. This is what loves does. He'll walk for miles in a trance, over fields and lanes of weirdish wild space. Steps over a dead fox without knowing it's there. In the end he'll reach a golf course and collapse on the green. Flat-out. A dark wind will roll over his face. The stars will be out and he'll look at them. He'll think about *me. What is he doing now?* Thinks about me so much and looks at the moon so much he'll feel his mind touch with mine. He is asleep and dreaming.

Inside this dream a tapping sound starts to wake him up.

The tapping sound comes from my fingers hitting these keys.

Writing his thoughts.

Making his mind up.

Skeletor

The city was full of moving people.

> He was in a doorway.
> Under a duvet.
> He looked warm under there.
> Little bearded head poking out the top.
> There was a Styrofoam coffee cup.
> Sometimes people threw coins in.
> Mostly they didn't.
> I did.
> "Thanks."
> "How's it going, friend?"
> "Alright."
> "Looks warm under there," I said.
> "It's alright."
> "Mind if I join you?"
> "What?"
> "It's fucking freezing out here. Mind if I join?"
> His eyes were watery and bloodshot.
> "Not really mate."
> "I'll give you twenty quid. Fuck it, *fifty*."
> He was tempted.
> "I'm not gay."
> "Me neither," I said. "Just want a warm."
> I took out two twenties and a ten.
> Put it in his cup.
> "Open up," I said, rubbing my hands. "I'm coming in."
> He opened up.
> I came in.
> His nails were yellow and black.
> It was fucking warm under there.
> People passed.
> Now my head was poking out and his head was poking out.
> The smell wasn't great but at least I was toasty.
> We didn't talk.
> Just stared straight ahead.
> The both of us/just the two of us.

You could see our breath.
　Mine.
　And his.
　Together.
　As one.
　It was then I noticed his duvet cover.
　It was colourful.
　Like a cartoon.
　There was a face.
　"Hey ain't that Skeletor?"
　"I don't know," he said.
　"Where's He-Man?"
　"I don't know what you're talking about?"
　I looked at Skeletor.
　He looked back.
　There was a quote underneath.
　Like a speech-bubble from his bony mouth.
　It read:

I am the Alpha and the Omega.
Death and rebirth.
And, as you die, so will I be reborn.

Sat with him for an hour.
People seemed to put less money in now there were two.
He'd done alright, though.
I'd say there was　　　　　　　　　　*profit.*

"Right. I'm off," I suddenly said, standing up.
He didn't say anything.

Just looked up at me.

I'm Out of Her League

Wearing odd socks.

    Wednesday on right.
Saturday on left.
Today is Tuesday.
For a while now I've had adoration for my neighbour's music.
It comes through the walls around noon and I enjoy it.
When I come back from the gym I find a fat girl on the doorstep so I say, "is that your music?"
She goes really red and looks really scared.
"Oh I'm *so* sorry."
"Don't apologise. I love it."
She can't tell if I'm being serious or not.
I am.
For once.
"Really?" she says, sheepish.
Goes even redder.
She's shaking a little.
"Want to come in for a cup of coffee?"
Straight away she slaps her forehead.
"Did I just ask a total stranger into my house?"
"I'm not a stranger," I say. "I'm your next-door neighbour."
I get déjà vu.
This is how I met Amber.
Similar script.
Minus the suicide attempt.
"I'd love to," I say. "Only I drink tea. A pot."
"You don't want much do you?"
"Not much in this life, no."
She lets me inside.
The flat is like mine.
Only in reverse.
And messy.
Much more messy.
There's a piano.
And other musical instruments.
"Can you play all these?"
She doesn't answer.

Dylan is on one wall.
Marley on the other.
Two Bobs, I muse.
She's wearing a dressing gown.
I look at her calves.
There aren't any.
"What do you do?" I ask, taking off my gym gloves.
"You mean work?"
"I mean whatever. Doesn't have to be work."
She starts to fill the kettle up.
"I don't work. I'm off work with depression."
"No room for small-talk. I like it."
"Sorry."
"No I like it. It's refreshing."
She raises an eyebrow.
"Depression is not refreshing."
"But your honesty about it is."
"Oh. Yeah. My therapist says honesty always. Depression isn't something to be ashamed of."
"Why you depressed?"
"Dad committed suicide."
"Snap."
"What?"
"Mine too."
"Really?"
She gives me a strange smile.
"Yep."
"How long ago?"
"I don't quite know. I'm not very good with time."
I look at the clock.
It's stopped.
She's made coffee, not tea.
But.
I'm cool with that.
This time.
She was probably distracted by My Looks.
"Mine was last year."
"How?"
"Pills."
"That's a woman's way."

"Is it?"
"Apparently."
"What about yours?"
I put an imaginary rope around my neck.
And pull.
"Hanging?"
"Yup."
I try to work out if she's fatter than Megan.
Nope.
She's not.
Maybe Megan two months ago.
"Sorry you wanted tea," she says suddenly.
"I did."
"Want me to make some?"
"Yes."
She looks shocked.
Makes a point of showing me the scars on her arms.
"Do you have biscuits?"
"Pardon?"
"Biscuits."
She starts to laugh. "You serious?"
"Fuck yeah I'm serious."
Now she really starts to laugh.
"I don't think I've met anyone like you."
"You won't have," I assure.
"You're not real."
"I know. Neither are you. We're just characters in a book."
Now she's smiling and laughing I see that she has a whole new face.

Pretty, bordering beauty.

Dark eyes.

Kind of cunning and lovely at the same time.

"I can send you my music if you like it so much."
"How?"
"Send you a link."
"I don't even know what that means. I don't understand technology stuff."
"Oh my."
"Maybe you could just make me a CD."
"This isn't 1998."

After my tea and her coffee we decide to play each other our favourite songs.

She plays some techno track and I play her … *She's like the Wind.*

She laughs so much she starts to cry.

She laughs through the whole song, all 3mins and 54 seconds of it.

"What are you laughing at?" I say.

"You're so funny. I haven't laughed like this in years."

At the front door we hug.

"Congratulations," I say.

"For what?"

"Your days of depression are a thing of the past."

"Are they?"

"Sure."

"And you know this how?"

Saying anything in this moment would spoil the effect.

So I don't.

Letter

Dear Hollywood,

Even tho were not in "an offishal" relationship I wanted to ask you if you wanted to go to lundon with me. Check this! I just found out that my ultimate icon and massiv inspirrationul figure is cumming to London to do a book singing on her new book of photography and i cant believe it! Check this! Ill make shor I spell her name right. CHLOE SEVIGNY is comeing to town. Un fucking reel. Xxxxxx im lirally bouncing thru the roof. With excitement im actually going to meat her in flesh and ill probly faint or something. shes the coolest woman on the planet and a stylish icon. Do you know her do you know her??? I no you don't rarely know about acters and actreesses and stuff and dont give a shit bout that but do you know her do you ACTUALLY know CHLOE SEVIGNY. Do you no who she is? Shes so beautiful in the weirdest way and kind of androgenus and sometimes looks like a boy and her eyes are dark and she has this sex appeel witch noone gets but everybody cant deny. As you can probly tell im all most freeking out right now so will you come to london with me. ITS on December the 12th will you come with me??I can get the book and sehll sign it and ill get to touch her skin and probably giv her a hug and u know me I belleve you only liv once so ill probably do some thing mad like try and give her my number becarse shes bisexul and ill never get this chance agen just imagine!! Sex with CHLOE SEVIGNY so ill probly write her a love letter and yowel havta ACTUALLY help me with that more obvius reesons. Will you write Chloe a letter for me? Will you cum to London ? I no u havnt got much money so ill paye willing to paye for all this exspenses and experience. Well have to stay over the night b fore because I want to be at the front of the que so well hafa get there early like at 6am or some thing because I want to be the first face she sees becarse if were late she mite get tired and ill be just anuther face in the crowd. As you can see I have planned all this out in my head. Don't think im a werid stalker or anything I just need to met CHLOE SEVIGNY.

So. Please say yes and ACTUALLY come with me becarse I don't want to go with anyone else.

Shes cool. So cool. Too cool. So ill need to be cool to be on her level and ur the only one who can keep me cool and calm like that.

So come with me to London.

If you don't know who CHLOE SEVIGNY is because shes kind of alternativ and not maynestreem like kate winslet or Cameron diaz or hally berry or anyone like that so go google her or watch one of her films so you will no who she is before you meet her./

HAAAA

Im exhausted now. Dog tired. May go drink sum alcohol sum wine to settel me abit. Shunt becuz of my meds but fuck it.

Ps they say you shunt meet your heroes but this time I don't ACTUALLY care ... xxxxxxx

CHLOE SEVIGNY.

Superman

My first confrontation with Greatness was when I was five year's old.

It was when Dad bought me a Superman mug.
　I had to tilt my head back to see it at the supermarket.
　That was the one I wanted, *Superman*.
　It stood out from all the other mugs.
　It was better.
　Bigger.
　Chunkier.
　More colourful than the rest.
　"Superman."
　Dad put it in the basket.
　When we got home Mum said,
　"Oh that is ridiculous. How is he supposed to drink out of that? It's bigger than he is."
　I hugged it and carried it around like a baby.
　The mug never lost value.
　Unlike all the other toys I got bored with after a few days.
　Superman stayed with me.
　Glued to my hand.
　I never really drank from it.
　Just swung it.
　Spun it.
　Filled it.
　Emptied it.
　Stared at it.
　Talked to it.
　Licked it.
　Tapped it.
　Sang into it.
　Loved it.
　"You're going to break that one day if you're not careful," Mum said.
　"What's break?" I said.
　"You'll drop it and it will smash, *break*."
　"I don't get it."
　"It means it will be no more."

When Mum left I became curious about *break*.
How could something just be *no more*?
Mum is a liar, I thought.
I wanted to test this so I dropped Superman on a cushion, *nothing*.
Threw Superman on a cushion, *nothing*.
Moved the cushion out the way, *nothing*.
Threw it on the carpet, *nothing*.
I noticed I was thirsty and my hands were beginning to shake.
I went into the kitchen and threw Superman on the tiled floor, *nothing*.
"Superman can't die!"
I put him on a shelf and pushed him off, *nothing*.
Again.
Nothing.
Again.
Nothing.
Threw him at a wall, *nothing*.
I wanted Mum to come in and stop me, take him away and put him somewhere safe.
I threw it harder and harder.
Nothing.
I wanted to kill Superman.
I wanted to beat him, prove it could be done.
Yet at the same time I was terrified to lose him.
Again.
Nothing.
I couldn't stop.
It was like there was something controlling me.
A force outside of myself.
I managed to climb up to the top cupboard.
Right on the ceiling.
It was crazy up here.
Everywhere looked dizzy.
I held superman up to the light.
Let him go.
I watched him spin in slow-motion, like a feather floating.
All the time looking at Superman's eyes.
Never left them.
He got smaller and smaller.

"What are you doing?"
My mum's voice came just before **impact.**
It was an explosion of a million, trillion pieces.
This was *break*
This was *no more*
Superman was gone.
I had killed him.

This was the last time I ever cried.

This was *officially* how my greatness started.

Her First Film

Watch another film with Chloe in. It's her first film, I think. She's younger in this one. Much younger. Almost a kid. She appears in more scenes than the other film. Guess she's the main character. Or one of them, at least.

Her name comes up in swirly red font against a black background. Camera swings in from the left and catches her face.

"I don't wanna speak to that dick."

Wears a blue t-shirt with white trim. Talks about the boy who stole her virginity. Her accent is street-thick. Heavy-eyed, she looks like a boy, as always. Chloe is in a room full of girls. They all talk about how bad boys are and how good boys are. She watches and listens and talks. They talk about sex and how they love it.

"Not sex, foreplay, foreplay," she says.

She is amazed and amused. The quietest of them all. Chloe says she hates sucking dick. They are her own words. It's the worst. She doesn't get anything out of it.

"No," she shakes her head.

Telly is the only guy she has ever slept with. They talk about AIDS. There is a red and pink and blue flower behind her. Chloe went to the clinic with her friend to get tested. She only went to keep her friend company.

A nurse asks how old she is.

"Sixteen."

She sits with her back to the wall. She is pale and dark-eyed. Wears a vest.

"How many people have you had sexual intercourse with?"

"One."

"Were you protected?"

"No."

"Have you ever had anal intercourse?"

She's embarrassed. Shakes her head. Smiles. "No." Looks down.

She waits in the waiting room for her blood results. This is a different day. She looks at the posters on the wall, a basketball player, a drawing with two people kissing, *you are not alone,* rows of multi-coloured condoms, each with a message inside. Her friend is talking but she's not really listening. Nurse looks at her through a glass door and picks up a file. Says her name. They sit down in her office. She hugs herself.

She has tested positive for the HIV virus.

"What?"

"The test isn't a 100% but ..."

"But I only had sex with Telly. I just came here to keep Ruby company."

Outside she makes a call from a phone booth.

"Peter is Mom home. No I need to speak to Mommy. Peter...where's Mommy?"

She is sixteen but sounds about twelve.

"No I can't talk to you right now...yeah...alright. Just tell her that...never mind."

She cries and breaks down in her friend's arms. The wind blows her hair. Trees are in the background. And a police siren. Or eerie music.

She has to go find Telly. She wants to find him alone. She runs through people and traffic. They watch her disappear down the street.

Later Chloe takes some steps and presses a buzzer and asks for Telly. A male voice asks if she wants to go upstairs and make-out.

"Yo I'm serious. Where's Telly?"

He's not there. He's downtown with Casper. She looks at a blonde baby holding a black doll.

She rides a cab. Staring out of the window. It's Chloe's face again. Cab has low-volume jazz music playing.

"Excuse me," the driver says.

His bushy eyebrows appear in the rear-view. "Can I ask you a question? I'm sorry I don't mean to be a pest."

His accent is strange. "I was looking at you and you look upset."

She does.

"I like looking at you. But your face looks upset."

The driver has a strange face to go with his strange voice. He wears a Hawaiian shirt. Smokes a cigar. "So I was wondering if I could be of any assistance. Maybe cheer you up or something?"

Her face is framed in the rear-view.

"No I'm okay thanks."

"You don't look okay," he says. "You are a very pretty young lady. But your face looks troubled."

"It's just been a bad day."

He scratches his big beard.

"Miss would I be prying if I asked what was wrong?"

"Everything's wrong," she says.

"Ah, not everything. The sun is still shining. It's a beautiful day out. Some things are okay, right?"

"Yeah, I guess so."

"Did you break up with your boyfriend?"

"No."

"Are you in trouble with the law?"

"No."

"Am I getting close?"

She unleashes her surprising smile. Just like in Real Life.

"That's better," he says. "You look like a prom queen when you smile."

He tells her a story about his crush on the prom queen. Says she looks a bit like her. Around the cheeks and the chin.

"Thanks."

He tells her that life is too short and she should try make herself be happy.

"What if you can't make yourself happy?"

He tells her to forget. His grandmother told him the way to be happy is not to think.

They drive under an ark.

"That's life."

She walks the streets. The day is beginning to fade. The Empire State Building can be seen in the background, only just. She kisses a friend and asks if she's seen Telly. She has. Telly and his friends have just beaten up some kid. Says Telly is going to some club called NASA.

She cuts the queue to the club. Meets a crazy kid with glasses who shows her some group sex in the toilets. Hands rub in the dark. After he gives her a present. Pops a pill in her mouth to forget. Just like the cab driver said. Her top is glow-in-the-dark.

"Don't you know tricks are for kids?"

She sits down with her head in her hands. Her friend wants her to dance. She can't. She doesn't feel well. She's fucking up in the club. Strobes and noise. She wanders through it eyes half-closed. Needs someone to rescue her from this day.

Takes another cab and looks out another window.

"I'm not going to die."

She cries. The city moves through her.

She enters an apartment block and takes a lift. She's wacked-out and spaced-out. Looks up towards the light. The lift rings with the passing of each floor. Her eyes are gone. They are not her own. Staggers down a green corridor with an exit sign behind her. Stumbles upon the aftermath of a party. Half-naked teenage corpses are littered across the floor. She searches for Telly. She needs to tell him the news. Only he's having sex with a 13-year-old girl in another room.

It's daylight.

She finds the room only it's too late.

"Shut the fucking door."

Her image is a featureless silhouette. Like the cover of *this* book.

It's the end of the day. She finds a spot on the couch. Hugs her knees and weeps. Eventually she falls asleep. A boy sits next to her sleeping body. Looks her up and down. Touches himself. Tries to wake her but she won't. Whispers in her ear.

"Wake up. It's me, Casper."

Touches her left breast. Kisses her. She moans in her sleep. Strokes her naked tummy. Rubs the outside of her jeans. A car beeps from outside. Starts to undo her red belt. She doesn't move. Pulls off her jeans and has sex with her. Rapes her.

"Hey it's me Casper."

Her feet are in the air, over each shoulder, white socks in the camera, moving back and forth. You can see her calf but there is no calf to see. Her legs are teen-thin. She groans but is still asleep. He tells her to *shush*. He repositions himself. The couch creaks. Her limp hand bumps lightly against his neck. He tells her not to worry. Her body is crushed and all tangled up. A plastic cup falls to the floor. Limp hand dangles some more. She has a ring on her finger.

Fade to black.

"Jesus Christ what happened?"

Letter

Dear Ms Sevigny,

I write you a formal fan letter although I hate that term, *Fan*. Puts me beneath you. Although I can think of worse places to be ☺
   Oh my god I can't believe I just emoji'd you.
   How embarrassing.
   Well. I can't believe you're here. Man. What a rush.
   My name is Amber Rice and I'm your biggest non-fan fan.
   Hopefully today I am the first face you see. If I am then I was the early bird catching the worm. Not that you're a worm, but, you get the gist. I've been advised to keep this letter short and simple and not to ramble. As I *have* been known to ramble, from time to time. Ideally I wanted to handwrite you this letter but trust me you'd probably need an interpreter to decipher my crazy scrawlings. Plus my spelling is *so* bad. I'm dyslexic. But that's another story.
   I'm also a photographer and I've just finished an exhibition not too far from here and I just want to say that your image and style and spirit and character has truly inspired me as an artist. And I think we should meet for a quick coffee before you head back over the pond.
   I have no agenda just want to be in your company for an hour or two.

   So, I leave you my number on the other side.
   Hope to hear from you.

   If not that's cool.

   Have a great life of love and laughter and keep on the good fight.

   Signed: *Amber. Xxxx*   *x*

Hotel

Hotel we're staying at is cheap and dingy and makes me think of skid row L.A. Already there is an angry man kicking-off at the receptionist on front desk.

"Taps! The taps are filthy, *disgusting*."

The Tap Man is really going for it, shouting, and everybody is looking. His hands are on his hips and his trousers hang-low and even his bald-patch is angry. It glows red like a traffic light on STOP.

"One is too tight and one is too loose. The cold spits out water and the hot isn't hot but *lukewarm*. It's just not good enough!"

It looks like he's been giving her shit for a while cos she looks drained and scared and about to breakdown crying. By the time we get to her she is seconds away from meltdown.

"Just to let you know," I come in grand and loud.

Her face is about to crumble.

"Just to let you know that the only reason we're checking-in today is because the last time I was here I was blown away by the supremacy of your impeccable taps. I just couldn't get enough of them and I'm back for more."

The girl, pretty and freckly, who moments ago was on the verge of chin-wobble tears just falls apart with laughter. Her whole body slumps into it and she does indeed cry a bit.

"Oh I love you!" she says. "That really has made my day."

She notices Amber behind me. "Oh sorry," she says, still laughing, wiping her eyes. "But your boyfriend has just turned a bad day beautiful."

Everyone is now laughing. Everyone is having a great time.

The only one who isn't is Amber. She hasn't taken any of it in.

None of it.

She is elsewhere.

Her mind is preoccupied with

Chloe Sevigny

Amber bounces up and down in my lap, waving the letter in my face.

"Baby that is perfect. You've *actually* got through *exactly* what I want to say without my mad ramblings yet you've not lost my vision at all. Thank you, thank you, thank you!"

People on the train look over.

"My testicle hurts."

"Sorry baby did I kick you?"

Amber talks all the way to London.

And on the tube.

And at the hotel.

And at the restaurant.

"I still can't believe you don't know her?"

"I don't."

"I still can't believe you haven't seen any of her films."

"I haven't."

Despite all the excitement she's asleep the minute her head hits the pillow.

As always.

While I'm left awake.

As always.

I'm tempted by *a wander*.

Maybe go see if the receptionist is still knocking about.

But the clock is set for six so I better not risk waking myself up any more.

I don't think I've ever woke at six in my whole life.

Ever.

At 2:46 my phone goes.

Ben.

"Hello."

It's more of the same only this time he's really incoherent.

Amber is right.

There's an edge.

And he's gone over it.

In the end I just sing him a lullaby until he sleeps.

Until *I* sleep.

Before I know it I have an alarm in my ear and an Amber bouncing on the bed.

"It feels like Christmas."

I sleep more while she showers and tarts up.

Getting out of bed at the very last second.

Amber stares at me.

"It's not fair. How can you roll out of bed at the last minute and still look like a million dollars?"

She's right.

I do.

Mirror flinches at my handsomeness.

I'm 6:3 today.

And that's without cowboy boots.

We hit the High Street and Amber becomes a mess.

She turns white and then vomits in a bush.

She's even more nervous than when she met me.

"Jesus Christ Amber it's a human being."

"I'm fucking up."

"I can see that."

"Give me some water."

I do.

"It's a human being," I repeat. "Get a grip. She's made up of the same shit as you and me."

"Okay," she says. "Okay."

She's back together again.

Amber's plan worked.

We're the first there.

But that was always going to be the case, arriving at this ungodly hour.

It's 6:45 and the doors don't open till midday.

That's over five hours standing by a glass door.

Moments later another set of stalker fans rock up.

Disgruntled that we beat them to the pole position.

They carry books and DVD's and wear t-shirts.

We wait.

And wait.

An hour later and a sizable queue piles up behind us.

Amber looks better.

More colour in her cheeks.

She's still quiet though, silent.

An Amber I have never seen before.

We take turns to leave the queue for snacks and toilet breaks.

Around 11 someone announces that Chloe Sevigny has entered the building and that's when Amber starts to fuck up again.

Vomit.

Nausea.

She can barely stand.

"I need to go. I'm gonna pass out."

"You're not going to get to meet her."

"I know."

"You've paid all this money and waited all this time."

"I'm so sorry."

"Don't apologise to me. You're the one who's going to miss out."

"I know. But I can't. It's just too much for me."

"It is kind of ridiculous."

"I know. I don't understand it. It must be the meds. It must be Chloe. I don't know. All I know is that if I don't leave I'm going to faint."

She's in my arms.

I'm holding her up.

"Let's go then."

"No!"

Amber comes back to life.

She holds my face.

"You need to stay."

"Why?"

"You need to meet Chloe. You need to give her my letter."

"No way. I need to look after you."

"*Please,*" she seems to yelp. "You're my only chance."

"Only chance of what?"

"Just – "

I laugh at the absurdity of all this.

She hands me the letter.

Her whole arm is shaking.

"Man," I say, looking at the crowd behind us.

She thrusts the letter into my chest.

"And make sure you touch her."

Shake my head.

Before I know it Amber has gone, staggered through the crowd like a wounded soldier.

Now I stand alone.

Alone with a glass door and a couple of thousand people.

Ten minutes later there is some movement in a window.

Some bland blonde wearing jeans and a t-shirt puts something in her ear and sits.

Is that her?

Can't be.

I look around for a movie star.

For a moment I think I could be in the wrong place.

A little smiley lady with a clipboard comes forward and unlocks the doors.

There's commotion behind me, bordering hysteria.

I stand there.

Two security men position themselves at either side of the table.

The girl sat at the centre of it waves me on, as if to say, *don't be shy*.

I step through the door and then the room seems to flash.

Gold and white.

Like the sun in my eyes.

When I get my vision back Chloe is right in front of me.

"Hi," she says.

We look at each other.

"You talk at last." I say.

She nods.

"Yes," she says.

We smile an easy smile at each other.

"So," she says. "This is where we meet? In *here*."

She looks around her.

I do too.

"Yup."

"Strange," one of us says.

We're silent for a long time.

"So what's fame like?" I ask.

"I don't really know," she says. "Most of the time I don't even notice. Suppose it's just a state of mind. Like everything else."

"Guess you have a kind of omnipresence," I say.

"Maybe. But no more than the mailman."

Her voice is deep and she kind of talks from the side of her mouth.

"Why did you choose *me* anyway?" she says.

"Ask Joe Cassius. He's the one writing all *this*."

They both look at me for an answer.

I can't really give them one.

They're no more arbitrary than Nicholas Elliott or the any number of *others* in here.

Chloe smiles and shakes her head.

"Anyway back to reality," she says. "You want a signed book?"

"Oh yeah. Almost forgot."

She takes one and signs it and hands it over.

"Thanks."

Her head is down and her eyes are up.

"Catch ya later Chloe."

"Catch ya later Our Hero."

I smile and sigh and roll my eyes.

Leave her there.

One of the security men points me through a side-door.

Back on the street I look down to see Amber's letter still in my hand.

"Shit."

I look back but the moment has passed and she's talking to someone else.

So I fold the letter up.

And slide it into the nearest drain.

Badlands

again always america all my life and your county becomes the english version of the midwest where the flatlands meet the badlands where martin sheen wears dean and where sissy plays it down plays it dumb plays it cool on these wide dry plains where slow tractors move across rickety bridges and it's like i'm in dakota all over again just like the last time just like last summer and the very height of it june thirteen and oh what a day that was the same day when cormac mccarthy died and mel ellis had her birthday and that crazy black man took to my streets with a blade and made the news made a rampage out of it all while my own mafia man chauffeured me directly to your front door only it was so perfect the way his wheels rolled to the right point in the road so when your door opened i couldn't see your face but could hear your voice and you opened it all up opened the book this book this page all bookmarked and beautiful and again your eyes roll over these words and again your eyes roll over these words and again your eyes roll over these words and again your eyes tell me that the fullness of life and art merge on the freeway and this is what happens when your eyes merge with the word with the word with the word with this weirdish wild space

James Dean

Met James Dean one time. Just the once. It was in 1975. Five years before I was born and twenty after his death. We met in a dream. I was lying on a blanket in the park, watching some teenagers playing football on the grass. I thought something was odd because they were wearing flairs and tight long-sleeved sweaters and they all had these big 1970's perms. I also noticed they were kicking the ball between jumpers instead of actual goalposts. Something wasn't right, out of whack. So I went over to a bin and pulled out a newspaper and the date at the top read, *Wednesday March 12th 1975.*

That's when I realised I might be in a dream.

I didn't want the dream to end so I walked around a bit, trying to stay awake/asleep.

And that's when I noticed an oncoming figure on the brow of the hill. The figure looked weary and kept rocking from side to side. As he got closer I noticed he had a big quiff of hair. As he got closer still I noticed he was wearing clothes from the 1950's. As he got even closer I noticed he was real handsome. As he got closer and closer, very close, I realised it was James Dean.

"Hey Jimmy."

"Where am I?"

He looked like he was ready to cry.

"People say you look like me."

"What?"

"You're in a dream my friend."

"A dream?"

"It's 1975," I said.

"Can't be."

"It is."

We talked for a bit.

"I haven't even been born yet," I said. "And you ... well you're dead."

Now he *did* cry.

I put my arm around him and gave him a little cuddle. I had to console him so I said, "but your work lives on. You became an icon in the eyes of the people and that's what you always wanted. Just drive a little slower, man."

"Okay." He said.

"Oh fuck it," I said. "Just go for it."

At that moment I saw my mum and dad through the window of a bus.

Then I woke up.

Ultimately, You Don't Care About Greatness

You're sitting up in bed, legs under the covers. Tea to the left, Buddha to the right. The sound of workmen working outside. Fingers tapping *these* keys. Even though this is only a short novel you're feeling a little exhausted. All this astral navigation has made your feet sore and your soul weary.

Really, you should think about wrapping it up, or start to wrap it up at least. Only you've still got shit to do, things to resolve. Ben needs closure. Chloe needs her calf touching and you're wondering how you can find a way to bring Swayze back.

All this and your mind is still on the audience, hoping they're having a good time, enjoying themselves. Getting their money's worth. More than anything you hope you're coming across okay. You hope that they're not taking this too seriously. You hope they're not taking *you* too seriously. You hope they see this for what it is, a comedy. A satire of the self. A trippy trip through the layers of The Self. You hope they see this casual narcissism as fun-poking at our own ego. You don't *really* believe that this is the 93rd Greatest Novel of All-Time. You're not sure if it's even the millionth.

Ultimately, you don't care about greatness.

Ultimately, you only care about love.

You want this to be a loving novel, almost like little paper arms could sprout from the side, reach up to the reader and *squeeze*.

So that this novel becomes a hug, a cuddle, a companion, a song, an ode to optimism, a candle in the dark, something to light the way ... lead the way ...

Shit. Sorry. See.

You're getting ahead of yourself again.

Just can't help yourself, can you?

Slow down. Pump the breaks. Back up.

Stop being so eager to please. Stop being so cringingly obsequious.

I know you try to act like you don't care what people think but *deep down* you do. Deep down you crave to be accepted, just like anyone else.

Anyway congratulations you've managed to waste yet another chapter talking about *nothing*. Time you got back to it, and not just back to the novel but the actual *story*.

People want a story so stop side-tracking.

And no more going on about Hollywood movie stars. The readers don't care, do you?

Ledger

I'm not saying it was as bad as when Swayze died (obvs) but the world did lose something when it lost Heath Ledger. No face in the history of cinema had a more mystifying and intensive expression as Heath. Swayze was an open book and an open heart. He was love.

Love, love, love.

Heath was a war zone.

A bomb that ticked.

Even as early as *10 Things I Hate About You* there was something unsettling about the artist. It was a performance that said: *okay audience I am playing a teeny rom-com heartthrob but don't get complacent, there are dark forces rumbling.*

And man did they rumble. He spat in our in faces and at our screens. And if he had lived any longer I believe he would have cranked it up, *even more.* Like Swayze he was more than just an actor. Swayze taught us how to love but Heath taught us how to hate. He pushed us when we didn't want to be pushed. He held up a mirror to our faces and said *this is who you are! Look, take a good look!* Now I'm not saying he was the most gifted actor. He wasn't. But what he was, was, *a confrontational* actor. Maybe the most confrontational actor of all-time. He had venom. Torment. Thunder. He was *a storm*. He forced us to turn inwards and say *Hey! This is Life!* When he died we all lost something. A bit of something. Something that we can't ever get back. Something that we can't put our finger on but know it's there. *Was* there.

Ledger.

Life hasn't been the same since.

Miss that guy.

CLF

I've only got about a dozen or so pages of Joe Cassius' *A Happy Orphan* to go.

Can't wait to find out what happens in the end.
I take seat at an *al fresco* coffee shop and start reading this chapter.
Only movement in my peripheries fucks up my concentration.
Look over book:
A group of mothers with their kids.
The mothers drink coffee and talk about motherhood.
Kids play in the sand.
On climbing frames.
Throw balls.
Run around in circles.
And zigzags.
A little brown girl sits on top of the wooden house.
An explosion of afro hair.
She waves at all the mums.
"Your Carleen has got beautiful hair."
"Gets it from Marcus."
The kids are laughing and having a great time.
One mother stands away from the others.
She is kneeling next to her kid.
Getting him ready to play with the rest.
It's as if she is giving him some kind of pep-talk.
I can't understand it because it's a hot day yet she is zipping up his coat and fixing his hat.
The kid doesn't like this.
He keeps pulling down the coat and knocking off the hat.
Soon the mum quits and lets him be.
The first person the kid looks at.
Is *me*.
Coffee cup pauses at my lip.
Under my breath: *what the fuck.*
He has the biggest head ever.
And in that head is a wonky face.
And in that wonky face there are cross-eyes and hair-lip and a scar slashed across his forehead like a lightning strike.

His jaw and lips and teeth are all fucked-up.
He keeps jumping up and down on the spot.
Making this weird, high-pitched moan.
A bubble of snot pops over his nose.
He is, quite simply, a crazy little freak.
He runs into the kids, full pelt.
He is faster than the other kids and they don't see him coming.
When they do they run for cover.
What is so heart-breaking is that the mother is pretending that none of this is happening.
That he is a normal kid going off to play.
That everything is alright.
It isn't.
It's fucking bedlam.
Carnage.
The kids are scared to death.
Terrified.
The games stop.
The park goes mad.
Proper havoc.
The Crazy Little Freak takes over the joint.
It's a shame because all he wants to do is play.
Have a good time.
He doesn't want to hurt anyone.
All the kids are gone.
Apart from one who is frozen stiff.
Her face is white and her eyes are huge and the Crazy Little Freak is jumping up and down on the spot next to her.
Screaming his head off.
Mothers run onto the park and re-group their kids.
Trying to calm them down.
They play polite by scolding them.
Telling them not to be *silly*.
CLF's mother cries, head in hands.
Other mothers console her.
The Crazy Little Freak screams on and on, at no one and nothing.
He doesn't give a fuck.
I hide my face behind *A Happy Orphan*.

The book is shaking.
So are my shoulders.

I really hope they don't see how hysterical I am.

"Only You Can Make All This World Seem Right"

You know who you are. You know who you are *by now*. You know who I'm talking to. You know *exactly* who I'm talking to.

Yes. *You.*

You have to realise that you are the reason I'm writing this in the first place. You are the reason I write anything. You are the reason I write. Period. With a full stop at the end.

As long as you admire *this* then that's all that counts. If you like this but the rest of the world hate it well then that's just fine by me. You're the only person I'm trying to impress. You are the only human being I am really trying to entertain. So really I guess I should call this novel *An Audience of One*.

If I had to choose the perfect symbol that embodies us it would be that of the Yin/Yang. Dark and light. Day and night. Fire and ice. Because your doubt and scepticism has allowed me to keep a real tight grip on life. It has helped me to keep my feet firmly on the ground so as I don't get ahead of myself.

So, see.

See this seminal work dedicated to you and you only, only you. Your life, your work, and your death.

An Audience of One

Joe Cassius

Dedicated to Patrick Swayze

"Patrick Swayze's star-sign is Leo. And that figures. For he has the heart of a lion."

Joe Cassius

Black Coffee

Black coffee, you've noticed, is starting to overtake tea and I'm not sure this is a good thing. This is down to my growing obsession with *Twin Peaks*.

Can we offer you gentlemen a cup of Joe?
Black as midnight on a moonless night.

I go into Starbucks at the stroke of noon.

The guy serving gets powerfully and painfully nervous when he sees me. Probably My Looks.

He has a ponytail on the top of his head, a bad lisp, and a misshapen body. His whole arm wobbles as he tends to my *Grande Americano*.

I sit and sip and replay the dramatic final scene in the *Twin Peaks* saga. Where Agent Cooper and Laura Palmer visit her childhood home. They go late at night and the woman who now lives there doesn't recognise a thing they are saying.

"Sorry to bother you so late at night," Agent Cooper says.

They walk back down the steps, onto the street where they have parked. Once there they slowly turn and gaze back up at the house. Cooper steps forward, stirred, troubled by something, "what year is this?"

Laura Palmer blinks hard and looks at the house one last time. A dark wind blows through her hair. An eerie moan of something in the background, before it all suddenly comes back to her. She screams so loud and so terrifying it breaks the Fourth Wall and breaks my television.

All the lights in her childhood home slam shut to another heart-stopping sound.

I am left staring into the blank, black screen, staring at myself, not knowing what is real anymore.

The Dramatic Final Scene

Out at night.

    Again.
    Feels like my last night on earth.
    Or first.
    You just can't tell.
    It's all out tonight.
    Moon.
    Stars.
    Breeze.
    The breeze has a steady rhythm.
    Almost as if the earth is breathing.
    In.
    And out.
    Everything is:
    clear.
    defined.
    Everything has its place and purpose.
    One single thing is connected to the next single thing.
    Where one thing ends, another begins.
    It's *all* here.
    Just for me.
    I have the night in the palm of my hand.
    And it has me in the palm of hers.
    We work well together.
    The night and I.
    We go *way back*.
    Centuries.
    I walk between trees.
    Between cars.
    Between houses.
    Through a gate.
    Through a bush.
    A hole in a hedge.
    A gap in the fence.
    Up a hill.
    Down a hill.
    Stop.

Go.
Look around.
Wait.
Watch.
See what comes next.
A fox runs through my thoughts.
Keep walking.
Down a hill.
Up a hill.
Breathe.
Stop.
Lie on a skateboard ramp and look *up*.
Gaze.
Branches swish.
Grass waves.
Blossom falls.
There are creaks and moans.
Whispers.
Silence.
It all comes out at night.
Everything but the people.
All but one.
Two
I see another at the foot of the path.
Apple Tree Lane.
Heading on up.
Walking.
Towards me.
It's a rare thing.
A rare sight.
This.
Here.
At this time.
It could be a ghost.
Wearing white and floating.
Gets closer.
And.
Closer.
Breeze turns to wind turns to gust.
Just, like this figure is being pushed towards me.

And *I* to it.
Magnets.
We meet in the middle.
"Hello Chloe."
She smiles.
Her skin shines.
She looks brand new.
Like she's been dropped through a cloud.
Then she surprises me.
Shocks me.
Leans in and kisses my ear.
Lips to lobe.
Her head tilts one way.
Mine the other.
We smile.
Her eyes blue in the dark.
Blonde in the dark.
White in the dark.
Light in the dark.
She takes my hand and we walk.
She's supernaturally warm.
Her hand like a bulb.
See her glow in the reflection of a puddle.
Shadow of her signature quiff.
She flicks it.
Like she did in the church the first time I saw her.
Like she does always.
We head past a hall.
Through roads and lanes and parks.
A graveyard.
A housing estate.
Block of flats.
Upstairs and down stairs.
Over a bridge.
Round a lake.
This is our night.
Her night and my night.
Her hand and my hand.
Palms pressed.
Our steps are the same.

Heartbeats and breathing, too.
We have the same pulse.
From nowhere we are at my flat and I don't know how we got here.
It just, *appeared.*
We stand in the mouth of my door.
Noses touching.
Our faces almost seem like one big face.
Her eyes go green.
Then red.
Brown.
Black.
Back to blue.
Opens her mouth.
I think she is going to talk for the first time.
Say my name.
Say it so you can *all* hear it.
But.
She doesn't.
Instead.
A kiss.
Not a kiss but a nearly-kiss.
Lips so close they burn.
She pulls away and looks away.
Something else is here.
Someone else is here.
There is a blue blur of a boy.
Before me.
At me.
Into me.
A crazy face full of tears.
Thin and fast and full of hate.
Full of pain.
Then I feel pain.
Or what I think is pain.
A bite.
For some reason I think of electricity.
It spreads and takes over.
Feel a slice of cold invade my heart.
Stomach.

Ribs.

Somewhere, *down there*.

All *this*.

In a split second.

This face before me.

It belongs to Ben.

I'd recognise it anywhere.

The first words out of his mouth are:

"You're not even that good-looking."

I look down.

There is a handle sticking out of me.

Guess the rest of it is *inside*.

"I told you man. I'm not to everyone's taste. Some people don't get what all the fuss is about. Guess you're one of those people."

Suddenly he looks down.

Sees the same handle.

"Oh my god I stabbed you!"

"It appears so," I say.

He's truly shocked by this.

"Oh my god!"

He looks ready to faint.

"Let's just keep calm," I say. "I'm sure there's a way out of this."

"I only wanted to scare you."

"A Halloween mask would have worked," I say. "But I got the point. *Literally*."

Blood is leaking all over my fingers.

"Does is hurt?"

"No it feels nice."

"Really?"

"You've stabbed me in the gut. Yes Ben, it hurts."

"Oh."

There's a moment of silence.

Like he doesn't know what to do.

"Shall I pull it out?"

Hand wraps around the handle.

"Think it's better staying in," I say, blood in the back of my throat.

He lets go of it again.

"I'm so sorry. I really didn't mean to do this."

He starts crying.

I've literally heard Ben cry more than a hundred times.

More than any other human being in my life.

I know his sobs verbatim.

"You know you're probably gonna hafta do prison for this," I say.

"I don't care. I don't care about me. I care only about *you*."

"You could say it was self-defence."

"I deserve everything I get."

"Just say *I* had the knife and *I* attacked you. Make out you're some Bruce Lee muthafucka. You could use Chloe as a witness. But you'll get fuck all out of her."

I slump.

"What can I do?" he screams.

"Just help me up. I need to do one more thing."

He does and I start to move.

On my heels.

Clicking to the beat in my head.

Sideways like a crab.

"What are you doing?"

"Death dance."

"What?"

"DD."

The handle moves one way.

Then the other.

I fall, laughing.

On my back.

Knife handle pointing perfectly at the moon.

Look down at my feet.

They're still moving.

Moonwalking in thin air.

Ben's face is a picture.

Suddenly the penny drops and he takes out his phone.

Life is beginning to leak out, leak away.

World gets narrow between my lids.

A letterbox of closing scenery.

Can hear Ben, only just.

Fessin-up.

Telling the three 9's everything.

"I've just stabbed a great man and a true artist of life!"

He's asking Chloe for the address but she remains her usual talkative self.

So in the end he takes off.
Searching for a road sign.
I am left alone with Chloe.
Her expression hasn't changed the whole time.
Guess you could call it love.
She looks at me with it.
Right back at her with the same stuff.
I never believed there was such a thing as *the one*.
Until *now*.
So maybe I guess you could find this book in the romance section.
Right next to *Wuthering Heights*.
You smile.
I smile.
We all smile.
Chloe smiles.
She turns away from me.
Faces the brick wall.
Kind of diagonal.
Stands on a step.
Etches up her long white dress.
Bit by bit.
Hooks her left foot around her right ankle.
On one leg.
She slowly rises.
Elevates.
The calf comes to life.
It emerges from the dark in high-definition.

This is it.

I put my hand there.
Here.
I touch it.
I touch it at last.
I hold it in the palm of my hand.
I hold it in the palm of your mind.

This is it.

This is the climatic scene in the novel.
Last scene in a movie.
Where Our Hero achieves what he set out to do.
All senses roll into one.
A light goes on.
As a light goes out.

And the last thing I have in this human world is:

Chloe's Calf As A Portal Into A Higher Dimension

My hand goes through it. In cosmic waves through her entire leg. Body. Face. I see myself through her eyes. I step out of her and stand to one side. Looking at the other me that is laying in a pool of bright scarlet on the doorstep. I touch my stomach. There is nothing there. No blood. No wound. There is nothing here and no one can see me. Chloe can't see me and Ben can't see me and my next-door neighbour and all the other neighbours who are now out on the street can't see me. I am bright, like an orb. My feet are off the ground and I could go higher if I wanted to. *You* can't see me. I'm *weightless*. People have hands over their mouths. One man holds a woman. Someone cries. Children are kept away. A dog barks. A black cat sits on the fence, coolly watching. There is an amber streetlight flickering. Soon I hear a siren, two sirens. They get louder.

Something is in the corner of my eye. A circle of light. Like a little sun. It shimmers and starts to expand. It looks like a sphere, an ark, a door. Someone, or something steps through it. It is a human form. Features slowly appear.

I use my hand to shade the light.

I see hair. A hairstyle.

"Swayze!"

He steps forward, surveying the scene. Looking at me. There is a calm heroism in his eyes.

"Alright man," he says with a nod of the head. His hair bounces. Then he walks over, struts.

"Patrick what's going on? I'm scared."

"You're dead."

"What?"

"There's no easy way to say it. You're dead, man. A dead man. Just got to face it."

I look at the scene again, ambulance and police pull into the street. Then from nowhere I start to cry. Crazy, deep crying. Like a whole lifetime of crying pouring right through me from the gut up. Swayze puts a hand on my shoulder, then takes me into his big loving arms.

"Let it out, man."

"I always knew you were loving Swayze. I've been telling *them* from the start. That you were the most loving actor of all-time!"

My voice is muffled but he hears me.

"Don't worry about that."

"And you're the *real* hero of this novel. Not me. I know this now."

"I said don't worry about any of this."

"Okay Swayze."

He nods.

"Hey am I a ghost?" I say, looking up at him.

He holds my face between his two hands and looks deep into my eyes. "We both are."

"I don't know how to be a ghost."

"I'll teach you."

Suddenly we float up, higher, looking down on everything.

Police put Ben in cuffs and place him in the back of a car. Amber appears from nowhere, running crazy down the street, screaming. Police keep her back from my body. Then she sees Ben in the car and tries to attack him. He has his head in his hands. All the time Chloe sits on the kerb, smiling, a sweet smile, staring at her calf.

"Life is good," Swayze says. "But death is better."

He takes my hand and we drift away from the chaos.

"Can we go McDonalds?" I say. "Could murder a burger. All this dying makes a brother hungry."

"We don't really eat out here, man."

"What do we do then?"

"We just sort of float around. Looking at things."

"That's okay. I can do that. I mean that's pretty much all I used to do when I was alive."

"Cool."

We head into the sunset. Although it's night.

into the omniverse ...

Swayze Dayz

Joe Cassius

Dedicated to Everyone

"I'm not afraid of death. I'm going home."

P.S

He

died.

Dead.
Funeral.
Cool coffin.
Black, like a piano.
Shiny.
Can see your face in in.
You look good, sharp.
Yep, since turning thirty your handsomeness has almost become offensive.
So glad you didn't check-out at 27 like you were going to.
So glad you stuck it out.
You step forward and look at the rest of yourself in the coffin.
Suits really suit you only you never get to wear them.
Of course everybody is crying, some hysterical.
Especially when they play the song at the end.
The one from the film *Dirty Dancing, (I've Had) The Time of My Life*.
It's not even the right song.
It's the wrong song.
The one he likes is where Patrick Swayze sings himself.
You kept telling Amber but she never listened.
Now it's on and you look at her confused, tear-drenched face and the penny drops…*ah, this isn't the one?*
Straight away it's your fault.
You see it in her expression.
Blame.
Anger.
Hate, maybe.
You take a closer look.
Yep.
Hate's definitely there.
We start to file out from the rows of seats.
All of us.
One by one.
Most of these people you don't even recognise.
Megan's mum performing her usual rendition of Dylan Thomas.
Rage against the dying of the light.

Ha.
He wasn't raging against it.
He was dancing with it.
I know.
I was there.
By the door Amber is at you.
Her face in yours.
"That wasn't the song."
You say nothing.
"I don't believe it. I don't fucking believe it."
She's walking around in circles, hyperventilating.
"He liked this little ditty too Amber. Relax," someone says.
Actually he wanted the 1990's classic *No Limit* by 2 Unlimited to be played as he was cremated.
That followed by Cher's *Love and Understanding*.
She grabs your wrist and stares so hard you can see your reflection in her eyeballs.
"C'mon Amber."
Megan's mum comes to the rescue.
But Amber isn't done.
"You didn't even cry. And you're wearing *a hat*."
You touch your hat.
Her face is shaking.
For a moment you think she is going to pass-out.
"A hat at a funeral! Your *own* soul-mate's fucking funeral!"
The *fucking* seems to echo.
People look over.
It's then you see me for the first time.
Stepping from my chair with a flick of my blonde quiff.
At first you think I'm a beautiful boy but then realise I was the girlfriend.
I join my ex-girlfriend Megan who has to stand at the back because she is too big for the chairs.
Why are you nervous?
You're never nervous, *ever*.
The feeling is so alien you wonder if you're coming down with something.
I'm the only one not crying.
Megan is.
As usual she produces some impressive tears.

For a moment you think I could be a ghost.

Amber is still going ballistic about the song and you wonder if she's forgot to take her meds.

"And I bet you're not even coming back to the gathering are you?"

"I am now," You say, looking at me.

You pull up to the hall that Amber has booked for the gathering.

Step out the hearse like you're a movie star or something.

Pulling strange faces.

Talking in a bad American accent.

"Where y'all goin now?"

I can hear you from here.

Now people have stopped crying and are queuing at the bar like it's a Saturday night.

There's lots of food.

Biscuits, especially.

Everyone is complimenting Megan's mum on her poetry performance.

She enjoys the adulation.

Giving a speech *about* her speech.

You disappear into the unisex toilets and come back out without your hat.

Not a hair out of place.

You try and act cool but you are looking for me.

Again you get that nervous feeling in your tummy so you sit.

Then it happens like it always does.

The people.

They come.

They come to you.

You don't do anything or say anything but they flock like crows at feeding time.

You'd be lying if you said you didn't like it.

You'd be lying if you said you did.

Like is not the word.

Love is the word.

Adore.

Revel.

Thrive.

For some reason they want your attention.

Need.
Crave.
Compete.
You are pulled and prodded.
Hugged.
Kissed.
Squeezed.
It's always been this way.
The less you do the more they want.
People look at you, amazed.
You chew gum.
Comb back your hair with two hands.
Occasionally you'll wink at someone.
By the time your glass is empty it is replaced with a full.
Before you know hours have passed and the DJ has become a good friend of yours.
Gone is all that dreary *Dirty Dancing* music.
Amber trying to right the wrong by having Swayze playing on repeat.
Blurred Lines bounces from the speakers and you hit the floor, ring around you.
Hat back on, cocked.
You move.
Clicking to the beat.
Spin on your heels.
Sideways like a crab, Moonwalk.
Crowd go wild.
Clap.
Cheer.
Chant.
"This is what he would have wanted," I hear someone say.
You dance with Megan's mum.
His sister.
Linda.
Kathy.
Sylvia.
April.
Swinging from one lady to another.
You almost whip off your shirt.
Only you see Amber slumped alone in the corner and really you

should show some respect.

By now you're dancing with Megan, her XXXL funeral shirt open to an AC/DC vest.

"You're incredible!" she screams through the music.

At this point I head to the ladies to powder my nose.

When I come back I can see you both talking about me.

She's telling you how shy and mysterious I am.

You want to meet me.

Only I don't dance.

"Ah-ah. No way," Megan says. "You'll have to come to *her*."

It kind of goes quiet and in slow-motion as you walk towards me.

I'm looking at the floor.

Hand across my mouth.

"Babe." Megan shouts even though I'm not her *babe* anymore.

And then I do my flick of the quiff.

Look at you, right at you, into you.

Hold out your hand and I take it, just.

"Hi," You say.

My smile surprises you.

"Megan has just been telling you about me. I mean, telling *me* about *you*."

I say nothing.

"You're Chloe?"

I nod.

"I'm sorry for your loss," You say.

I look at the party behind you, then back at your face.

You no longer feel like a movie star.

It's like I can read your mind.

It's Like I Can Read Your Mind

That would have been the perfect sentence to end this with. *It's like I can read your mind.* I was going to leave it *there*. Instead I'm going to end it *here*. Reason being I want a chance to thank you. *Personally.* Thank you for all you have done. Because without you none of this would have been possible. You've stuck by me throughout. All the way from start to finish.

We made it.

We made it *this far.* And I can't ever forget that.

So, wherever you are *right now.* Whether it's sat in a chair or lying in bed, riding the bus or chilling in the park. Know that I'm thinking of you, *always.*

We'll meet again one day, I know. So, if ever you see me don't be a stranger. *I mean this.* Come over and tap me on the shoulder and simply say, "Hey." And I'll respond by taking you lovingly into my arms.

Really, I will.

After that we can go wherever you want. Moon and back.

Now it's time. Time to say goodbye. Like the song. In a little under half a minute you'll close this book and we'll go our own separate ways. But before you do I want you to do one last thing. Once the book is shut I want you to close your eyes and just do *nothing.* Breathe. Listen. Absorb all *this.* The moment. *Our* moment. Let the world wash through you. Keep your eyes closed and *feel* me. My mind touching your mind. Then open your eyes and take a look around. I will be out there, here, somewhere, *everywhere.*

CAST

(in order of appearance)

Joe Cassius .... himself.
Joe Archer .... himself.
Oscar Wilde .... himself.
George Orwell .... himself.
F. Scott Fitzgerald .... himself.
Solemn Russian Boys .... themselves.
Dr. Seuss .... himself.
Our Hero .... myself.
Mum .... herself.
Diana Ross .... herself.
Luther Vandross .... himself.
Dad .... himself.
Aunt Aud .... herself.
Liza Minelli .... herself.
Dylan Thomas .... himself.
People .... themselves.
Chloe .... herself.
Megan .... herself.
AC/DC .... themselves.
Matthew McConaughey .... myself.
DJ .... himself.
Justin Timberlake .... myself.
Sister .... herself.
Linda .... herself.
Kathy .... herself.
Sylvia .... herself.
June .... herself.
You .... yourself.
Unc .... himself.
Paper Boy .... himself.

House Spider .... himself.
Ex Miners .... themselves.
Margaret Thatcher .... herself.
Priest .... himself.
Ryan Gosling .... myself.
Amber .... herself.
Tom Cruise .... myself.
Danish Dude Lars .... himself.
Colin Farrell .... myself.
Jude Law .... myself.
Zac Efron .... myself.
Heather Graham .... herself.
Ted Bundy .... himself.
Lindsay Lohan .... Amber.
Emma Stone .... Amber.
Dwayne Johnson .... myself.
Days of The Week .... themselves.
Kids .... themselves.
Leonardo DiCaprio .... myself.
Patrick Swayze .... himself.
Bugs n' Flies ....themselves.
Spider .... herself.
Waitress .... herself.
Old Blind Nipple Woman .... herself.
Son Michael .... himself.
Christian Bale .... myself.
Richard Ramirez .... himself.
Harold Shipman .... himself.
Diane Arbus .... herself.
Ben .... himself.
Black Cat .... herself.
English Cows .... themselves.
Alec Baldwin ....himself.
Jennifer Love Hewitt Fan .... himself.
Jennifer Love Hewitt .... herself.
American Security Guards Pt 1 .... themselves.
Robber with Knife .... himself.
Breath Boy .... himself.
Tuesday Afternoon People .... themselves.
Daniel Craig .... Robber with Knife.

American Cows .... themselves.
Dead Squirrel .... itself.
Toothy Fuck .... himself.
Tommy .... himself.
Jerry .... himself.
Jerry's Wife .... herself.
Puck .... himself.
Bret Easton Ellis .... himself.
An Audience .... themselves.
Guy Next To Me .... themselves.
Jimi Hendrix .... himself.
Janis Joplin .... herself.
Brian Jones .... himself.
Kurt Cobain .... himself.
Amy Winehouse .... herself.
Victim .... himself.
Grief-Stricken Mother .... herself.
My Own Son Who Hasn't Been Born Yet .... himself.
Emilio Estevez .... himself.
Rob Lowe .... himself.
Demi Moore .... herself.
Ally Sheedy .... herself.
Judd Nelson .... himself.
Andrew McCarthy .... himself.
Andie MacDowell .... herself.
Cat .... himself.
Bradley Cooper .... myself.
White Horse .... itself.
Nicholas Elliot .... himself.
Ferris Bueller .... himself.
Taxi Driver .... himself.
Waiter .... himself.
Andy Warhol .... himself.
Elvis Presley .... himself.
River Phoenix .... himself.
Remy LaCroix .... herself.
Jason Momoa .... myself.
Madonna .... herself.
Another DJ .... himself.
Leonardo da Vinci .... himself.

Ludwig van Beethoven .... himself.
Sir Isaac Newton .... himself.
Galileo Galilei .... himself.
Singing Soulful Binman .... himself.
Young Hairy Policeman .... himself.
Dead Man .... himself.
Spoilt Kid .... himself.
Spoilt Kid's Mam .... herself.
Gerard Butler .... myself.
Russell Crowe .... myself.
Jason Statham .... myself.
Escort .... herself.
Peter Sutcliffe .... dad.
Yoko Ono .... mum.
Tom Sawyer .... himself.
Jane Eyre .... herself.
Holden Caulfield .... himself.
Denzel Washington .... Joe Cassius.
Forest Whitaker .... Joe Cassius.
Cuba Gooding Jr .... Joe Cassius.
Michelangelo .... himself.
Ryan Reynolds .... myself.
Ashton Kutcher .... myself.
Man Boss .... himself.
Woman Boss .... herself.
Work Colleagues .... themselves.
Justin Bieber .... himself.
Pizza Delivery Boy .... himself.
Jack Nicholson .... myself.
People in Cars .... themselves.
Magic Bus Girl .... herself.
Fat Chinese Woman .... herself.
Clapping Bus Person .... herself.
Another .... himself.
Bus Driver .... himself.
Bus Babies .... themselves.
Christian Slater .... himself.
Homicidal Bus Boy .... himself.
Offended Man .... himself.
Woman Feeling The Injustice .... herself.

Jenna Jameson .... herself.
Myra Hindley .... herself.
Joe's Mum .... herself.
Muhammad Ali .... himself.
Fake White Grandpa .... himself.
American Security Guards Pt 2 .... themselves.
Dead Fox .... itself.
Salvador Dali .... himself.
Virginia Woolf .... herself.
Mick Jagger .... himself.
Raphael .... himself.
Your Mum .... herself.
Nurse .... herself.
Broken Black Husband .... himself.
Nearly Dead White Wife .... herself.
O.J. Simpson .... Broken Black Husband.
Rosanna Arquette .... Nearly Dead White Wife.
Robert De Niro .... myself.
Al Pacino .... myself.
Ladybird .... itself.
Old Limping Man .... himself.
Voice Behind You .... itself.
Treadmill Girls .... themselves.
Sylvester Stallone .... myself.
Paul Newman .... myself.
Other Men .... themselves.
Black Girl .... herself.
White Girl .... herself.
Aggressive Alpha .... himself.
Waitress .... herself.
Jeremy Kyle .... himself.
Holly Willoughby .... herself.
Blind Woman .... herself.
Guide Dog .... himself.
Homeless Man .... himself.
Skeletor .... himself.

*Artwork, page 204, by Heba Rashed.

Depressed Neighbour .... herself.
Bob Dylan .... himself.
Bob Marley .... himself.
Chloe Sevigny .... herself.
Kate Winslet .... herself.
Cameron Diaz .... herself.
Halle Berry .... herself.
Superman .... himself.
Girls .... themselves.
Nurse .... herself.
Ruby .... herself.
Blonde Baby .... herself.
Strange Taxi Driver .... himself.
Friend .... herself.
Crazy Kid with Glasses .... himself.
Another Friend .... herself.
Half-Naked Teenage Corpses .... themselves.
Telly .... himself.
Casper .... himself.
The Tap Man .... himself.
Pretty, Freckly Receptionist .... herself.
Stalker Fans .... themselves.
Smiley Lady with A Clipboard .... herself.
American Security Guards Pt 3 .... themselves.
Martin Sheen .... himself.
Sissy Spacek .... herself.
Cormac McCarthy .... himself.
My City's Summer Spree Killer .... himself.
My Own Mafia Man .... himself.
Insects .... themselves.
James Dean .... himself.
Heath Ledger .... himself.
Mothers .... themselves.
Kids .... themselves.
Carleen .... herself.
CLF'S Mother .... herself.
CLF .... himself.
Starbucks Guy with A Crush .... himself.
Agent Cooper .... himself.
Laura Palmer .... herself.

The Woman Who Now Lives There .... herself.
Bruce Lee .... himself.
Neighbours .... themselves.
Black Cat .... itself.
Police .... themselves.
Everyone .... ourselves.